The Real Story

Sienna Waters

Published by Sienna Waters, 2020.

This is a work of fiction. Similarities to real people, places, or events are entirely coincidental.

THE REAL STORY

First edition. November 26, 2020.

Copyright © 2020 Sienna Waters.

ISBN: 979-8227160256

Written by Sienna Waters.

To N.–
Keeper of my secrets
xxx

Chapter One

Elle shifted her dark glasses against the bright lights of the meeting room. The one advantage of working for a women's magazine was that the glasses were seen as a fashion choice, rather than the inadequate protection that they actually were.

"But that's bullshit. Of course it's cheating. I mean, a text message without the pics, maybe, but with the pics, and those emoji choices, you'd have to be an idiot not to see it," Leila was saying.

"Which is why it makes a great article," said Charlie, patiently. "There's a line there somewhere, but where is that line? What's cheating for one person might not be for another. See what I'm saying here?"

Leila nodded thoughtfully. She was an intern. Young, naïve, occasionally stupid, but very, very eager. And one day, Elle thought, she was going to take her rightful place at the editorial table. Alongside Charlie, who'd probably been born with a glossy magazine in her hand and had been made love and relationship editor last year despite being six months younger than Elle. Not that there was any jealousy there.

"Right, that's settled then," said Kim with a brisk nod in Charlie's direction.

Elle shrank further down in her chair, praying like hell that Kim wasn't turning to her next. Her stomach trembled a little as Kim's eyes moved her way but stopped just short. She gave a boozy sigh of relief.

"Fashion and beauty, what have you got for me for this month?" barked Kim.

The tequila had been a mistake, she was willing to admit that. Well, the third one had. The first two had been warranted because, well, because it was Sunday night and who the hell liked Sunday nights? And because of the scandalized look on Buzz's face when she'd ordered the shots.

"On a Sunday?" Buzz had screeched over the pounding of the music. "What about your editorial meeting in the morning?"

"Editorial, schmeditorial," Elle vaguely remembered saying as she upended the first shot.

Her head banged like someone was chipping away at her brain with a hammer and chisel. It had been a jackhammer before the three ibuprofen she'd sunk as the meeting was starting. Stupid meeting. Stupid magazine. Stupid world.

Her stomach flipped again and she was wondering whether or not she was going to regret the greasy bacon and egg sandwich she'd picked up on the way to work. Grease to soak up the booze had been her plan, but now she could taste ketchup at the back of her throat.

"Elle, you're up."

She swallowed quickly, hoping she wasn't going to puke all over the table in front of everyone.

"Well, what have you got?" Kim asked impatiently.

Elle flicked through the notebook that she knew was empty.

Edina wasn't the bestselling women's magazine in the country. Hell, it wasn't even in the top five as far as Elle knew. It was a glossy, fat, slick pile that slid onto her desk once a month filled with beauty shots and articles that had been written months ago and forgotten about. Forgotten about because for the most part nothing about the articles was memorable. It was brain candy, Skittles or caramel popcorn for your head as you waited for the dentist to call your name in the waiting room.

Every eye at the table was on her. The three other writers, the editors, and finally, the editor in chief, Kim Lytham. Kim had once been a big deal at *Vogue*, or so the rumor went.

Elle racked her brains as Kim's face darkened until finally she managed to dislodge the kernel of an idea.

"Taylor Hadeen," she started, unsure of how the sentence was going to end.

Not that it mattered, because Kim's face was darker still. "Third rate reality TV stars? No, thanks. Next?"

Fuck. There hadn't been a first, let alone a next. She coughed to cover a pause and pulled the first name that she could think of out of thin air. "Deanna Deacon."

"Soap stars are so last year," said someone that Elle suspected was Leila.

Kim growled and began tapping her pen on the desk. Elle felt the blood pumping to her cheeks as she squirmed under Kim's gaze. She'd do better next week, she promised herself. Next Sunday she'd spend all afternoon working on her pitches and wouldn't drink anything stronger than tea. Probably. Maybe a glass of bubbly to celebrate having a list of fantastic ideas afterward. That would be fair, wouldn't it?

"Pitch me again over email by end of day," Kim said now. "I don't have time for this. Alright, everyone out, meeting done."

Chairs scraped over the carpet and Elle felt every muscle in her body relax. Her head was starting to feel better. Stomach too. In fact, now that she thought about it, she could really use a coffee. She scooted out of the meeting room before Kim could catch her eye.

HER FINGERS FLEW OVER the phone screen, typing out messages almost faster than she could read them.

think i might curl up and die from tequila poisoning. Meeting go ok?

Poor Buzz. She definitely needed to work on her tolerance. Elle frowned as she wrote back.

bit shit. think tequila erased all my pitches from my brain.

She barely had to wait a second before the reply hit her phone.

like you had anything prepared. ever considered taking your job seriously?! i'm not paying your half of the rent if you get fired.

Elle rolled her eyes. As if.

i won't get fired. trust me. i'm too loveable to fire.

Her desk phone rang just as she hit the send button. She picked it up without thinking, one hand still on her mobile.

"Elle, my office. Now."

No hello, no name, no nothing. Not that Elle needed Kim to identify herself. She'd hear that voice in her nightmares.

And all of a sudden she wasn't quite as sure of herself. Truth be told, she hadn't been sure when she sent the text to Buzz. Kim might fire her. Kim was pretty close to firing her, if she was completely honest. And it wasn't just the partying and the lack of article ideas. Even stone cold sober after a full night of sleep Elle knew she wasn't on a par with the other writers. Even writing someone else's idea, she knew she'd have four rounds of edits to do before Kim found the article acceptable.

She just didn't have the knack of it. Whatever that knack was. Six months ago she'd thought that she'd figure it out. Getting hired by her first magazine, how hard could magazine writing be? It was hardly the quickfire, high pressure world of newspapers, was it?

She slid her dark glasses back on. Newspapers. She'd already been fired by three of those. Had already accepted that newspaper journalism just wasn't her forte, which was fine. There had always been the idea of magazines lurking in the back of her brain.

But now, as she got up from her desk and slowly made her way to Kim's office, now she was worried. Just a little, just a niggling sense at the back of her brain, a little voice telling her that maybe this wasn't for her either, maybe she didn't have what it takes after all.

Except there were no other options. Nothing else she could do.

"Close the door," Kim barked as Elle walked in. "And take off those damn glasses. Let me see your face."

Elle did as she was told and then sank into the chair opposite Kim's desk. She couldn't get fired. Not from here. Not like this.

"You're walking a thin line, lady."

She took a deep breath, nodded, couldn't find words.

"I took a chance on you, a chance that I'm starting to regret. You do understand that you're supposed to present ideas for each issue, right?"

Elle nodded.

"Then what's the damn problem? Do I just need to fire you right now? Get you out of my hair?"

"No!" Finally, a word escaped.

"Then give me one good reason why I shouldn't."

And now that one word had escaped she couldn't stop the others. "I'm working on something. Something big. A profile piece. Huge. I just didn't want to mention it until the details had been ironed out, didn't want to disappoint if it didn't come through, I just…"

She stopped only because Kim was holding up a hand like a traffic cop.

"A profile piece?" Kim's voice sounded less harsh now, more… interested.

"Uh-huh."

Where the hell had that come from? Why the hell had she said that? There was only one question that Kim could possibly ask now, and she was damned if she had an answer for it. And she needed an answer. A good answer. No, strike that, a brilliant answer. Because only a brilliant answer was going to let her keep her job.

"A profile piece about who?" The obvious question.

Elle reached into her brain and wrenched out the biggest, most impressive name she could think of. The most unattainable, most private subject she could come up with. She opened her mouth and the name just spilled out.

"Alya Goldstein."

Kim's jaw dropped and Elle felt a thrill of satisfaction at the reaction.

Chapter Two

She drummed her fingers on the desk top, listening to the man's excuses. It was taking every last shred of her patience not to bang the phone down, but she held her temper. Outbursts and tantrums weren't her style, never had been.

Her nails needed a manicure. Neat and usually short, polished but not colored, they were getting longer than she liked them. She took a breath, closed her eyes for a moment and then, finally, the man took a breath. Time to jump in.

"I appreciate that you had issues," she said, politely but firmly.

"I did. But they won't happen again. I've got—"

"Which is exactly what you said last time," Alya said, staying firm. "Which is why we'll no longer be needing your services."

"But... But..."

"Please send your invoices to the normal address, I'll ensure that it's paid in full." She didn't wait for anything further before hanging up the phone.

Job done. Except now she needed to find a new supplier. Nothing big, just the little cards that doctors and hospitals dropped into patient information files, making sure that her potential clients knew that she existed. But still, it was one more thing to add to her growing list of things to be dealt with.

Not that the list was ever short. Owning and running a company didn't exactly leave much time for anything other than business. A treadmill in the corner of the office bore witness to this, a single, neatly folded towel hanging from its rail. She couldn't remember the last time she'd used it. Lucky that she had a fast metabolism, or at least that she skipped several meals a week due to work.

She leaned back in her chair and sighed. Her home office, like most of the rest of her home, was minimalist and quiet, white and pine and light and soothing. She needed all the help she could get in the soothing department.

A pile of papers sat in front of her and her laptop was open to a spreadsheet with multiple tabs and she rubbed at her eyes, numbers dancing in front of them.

MedSend was her own brain-child. She was CEO and CFO, and did whatever needed to be done, though the company was growing faster than she'd ever imagined. More than a hundred employees on the books and she was looking at yet another expansion. Not bad for a business that was just turning three years old. Not that this was her first rodeo, but still, it was her first big success.

The idea was simple. An app and telephone service that would make sure medications got delivered to those who were incapable of picking up those meds themselves. The disabled, the elderly, those too sick to get out. They called or texted or pressed a button on their app, and MedSend took care of the rest.

A simple idea, but there was more involved than most people imagined. Matching patients to valid prescriptions and weeding out those trying to illegally receive prescription drugs was just one problem. One that grew as scammers became more creative.

Still though, MedSend was doing well. Doing well didn't necessarily mean big profits though.

She glanced down at the clock on her laptop screen. About time, she figured. She rolled her shoulders and stood up, leaving the quiet of her office and walking down a long corridor.

There were awards, plenty of them. Not that she really looked at them. The interior decorator had somehow found the certificates and statues and whatever else and thought them the perfect decoration for the long hallway. There was one though, one that made her smile every time she saw it.

Young Female Entrepreneur of the Year, said the magazine cover. But that wasn't what Alya liked about it. What she liked was the black shadow outline of a head, a perfectly anonymous silhouette. Anonymous because she'd refused, just as she always did, to be photographed, interviewed, or even quoted in the ensuing article.

She made a rule of never, ever, letting the press into her life. They should have better things to do, in her opinion, than talking to someone who was just trying to mind her own private business and help a few needy people as much as she could.

"Bubbale!"

Stepping over the threshold into her grandmother's self-contained apartment always sent Alya spinning back through time. The smell, the colors, the furniture, it was like her grandmother's tiny Bronx house had been air-lifted into the apartment building. Her feet scuffed onto carpet, thick and swirled with pattern, a far cry from the polished floorboards just outside.

"Hey, Bubbe, I just came to say goodnight."

Her grandmother had already pinned up her grey curls and covered them with a hair-net. She was sitting, legs stretched out, on an armchair, a book by her side and a mug of cocoa on the table.

"You're still up working." There was a slight accusatory note there.

"I am, Bubbe. But I won't stay up too late."

Her grandmother tutted in disbelief. "You need someone to look after," she said. "That would keep you away from your desk."

"I have you," Alya pointed out.

"Then you need someone to look after you. And don't say you have me, you know what I mean."

Alya grinned. "Nobody would ever take care of me as well as you."

The words had their desired effect as her grandmother grunted and tried to hide her pleasure. "Still though, you should think about a family. How am I going to have great-grandchildren with you sitting around in your office all day?"

"Given that I'm gay, great-grandchildren might be a stretch," Alya said, having heard this conversation far too many times before. "And anyway, you're as proud of MedSend as I am, so you can stop that nagging about work right now."

Her grandmother smiled and nodded, a mosaic of wrinkles spreading across her face. "You do good, Bubbale. You help people. That's important in life. You give back, and I'm proud of you, you're right. I just worry about you sometimes is all."

"And I worry about you," Alya said. Her grandmother's face creased into a frown now. "Did you take your meds already?"

"I rattle like a pill-box every time I turn over in bed," grumbled her grandmother.

Alya took that as assent. "And your blood sugar? What was it the last time you checked?"

Shoshanna sighed the kind of deep, heart-wrenching sigh that only a Jewish grandmother can achieve. But Alya was having none of it. She went into the small bathroom and came out with a testing kit.

"Finger," she ordered.

One, shaking finger was extended and quickly and efficiently Alya did the test.

"130, not bad."

"See, even grandmothers can behave sometimes."

Alya laughed and bent to kiss her grandmother's cheek. "Good night then. Love you, Bubbe."

One hand reached out and grasped hers. "I love you too, little one," Shoshanna said. Her eyes were dark and bright like a bird's. "But there's plenty more love in the world, if only you'd go out and find it."

Alya just about stopped herself from rolling her eyes. Her grandmother wasn't about to let the subject go tonight. "You worry about your blood sugar, let me worry about my love life."

"I would if I thought you'd actually worry about it."

Alya laughed and left her grandmother to her bedtime routine. Work was calling her. She went back down that long hallway, the rest of the apartment silent and dark now. Empty. Not that she'd ever felt the need to fill it, much to her grandmother's chagrin. No, family, kids, relationships, not exactly her style. She was as anonymous as that black silhouette on the magazine cover and perfectly happy to remain that way.

DESPITE WHAT SHE'D said to her grandmother it was long after midnight when she finally shuffled her paperwork together and shut down her laptop.

The numbers were no longer swimming in front of her eyes, they were in orderly rows now, and she was absolutely clear on how everything added up.

MedSend was doing fine. Not about to go bankrupt, but then not about to make a killing either. And the growth rate was falling much faster than she liked to see.

Which meant only one thing. Expand. Get bigger. The bigger the risk, the more potential profit there was. And profit meant more money that she could plow back into the app and phone services, which meant she could charge a lower commission on meds delivered, which meant she could help even more people.

Ideally, those ordering delivery meds shouldn't be charged for the privilege at all. That had always been Alya's plan. Getting to the point where she didn't need to charge was the problem though. She'd skimmed as much as she could, pushed the numbers, manipulated data, and those delivery charges were as low as she could get them.

Making them zero though? That would mean expanding out into whole new areas, getting a whole new string to her bow, an additional service that could help fund the med delivery arm of the business.

Go big or go home, wasn't that what they said?

And it was time now to go big.

Alya's heart beat a little harder at the thought. Yes, it was definitely time to start taking more risks.

Chapter Three

"**I** fucked up."

"Tell me about it," Buzz said, sliding into the booth with a groan. "Tequila and beer on a Sunday night? Never again."

Elle grinned, not exactly what she'd meant. Besides, Buzz looked like she always did, like she'd just stepped out of one of *Edina*'s fashion shoots. With her half shaved hair, punk boots and artful make up, Buzz did something in PR. Something that Elle had never quite pinned down the details on, but a job that gave Buzz the freedom to pretty much do as she pleased as long as she went to parties, concerts and whatever other events her firm could dream up.

Buzz was also her best friend, flat-mate, and confirmed drinking partner.

"Another Jack and Coke," Elle shouted over after getting the waitress's attention.

Not that either of them needed it. But ordering a drink was just what she did. What they both did. It was part of the lifestyle, part of living in the city, part of who they were. And she was going to take it easy tonight, she'd promised herself that. Okay, so it was a promise that had been made before, but this time she was going to keep it.

"So how exactly did you fuck up?" Buzz asked.

Elle had a sudden memory of sitting in Kim's office. An icy feeling trickled down her spine. She slurped down the rest of her drink, feeling the warm alcohol in her bones and shouted over to the waitress: "Make that two!"

So much for taking it easy. Tomorrow would be alcohol-free, she promised herself. Wednesday too. That was fair. Two nights of drinking in trade for two nights of abstinence. Abstinence. Hmm. Across the bar the woman Elle had been watching tossed her hair back, baring the long, sleek line of her throat. Tall, dark, gender neutral, just the way Elle liked her partners.

"Hey, Earth to Elle! My face is over here!"

She tore herself away from the vision across the bar. Buzz was raising an eyebrow at her. "So, I fucked up," she said again.

"So you said. How exactly?"

And that stupid icy tremor went down her back again. "I, um, might have told Kim that I've got a profile piece that I'm working on."

"When you don't?"

"When I don't," Elle agreed as the waitress slid two drinks across to them.

Buzz sighed and shook her head. "Elle, sweetie, as much as I love you, have you ever really considered, well, not doing this?"

"Not doing what?" Elle asked, taking a long sip from her drink. "Not fucking up? I mean, sure, yes, I try."

"I mean maybe taking life seriously once in a while," Buzz said.

Anger prickled her skin. "Like you do? With all your partying?"

"That's my job, Elle. And yours, in case you've forgotten, is supposed to be journalism. Which, if we're being very, very honest with ourselves, might not actually be your thing."

"Of course it's my thing. What are you talking about? I've got a damn degree in it and everything."

Buzz sighed and took a small sip of her own drink. "Do you like your job?"

"Yes, obviously."

And she did. Kind of. She liked telling people what her job was. She liked the idea of her job. It was just... the actual work part of it that she wasn't terribly fond of. But then people had jobs they didn't like all the time, didn't they? And it wasn't like she had a ton of options. What else was she supposed to do?

"If you really do like your job, then you're going to have to start taking it more seriously. Putting a little planning into your pitches. I'll be your sounding board if you like. I can even help come up with ideas."

And Buzz's blue eyes were soft and kind and Elle couldn't be angry with her.

She'd walked into a college dorm nearly fifteen years ago now, leaving her parents behind. They'd only had time to drop her off and ditch her stuff on the side of the parking lot before they'd both had to get back to work. And she'd been feeling lost and sad and so very alone. Even though all she'd wanted for the last couple of years was to get out of the house, to get her life started.

And then a head had poked up from the top bunk bed, complete with pink spiked hair and a barbaric looking pin through the nose, and an oddly cultured voice had said: "Hi, I'm Buzz. Who are you?"

Fifteen years. Through college, through boyfriends and girlfriends and jobs and moving and everything else. Buzz had always been there for her. On the absolute worst day of her life, when she'd hung up on her father with her hand trembling, Buzz had been holding her other hand. Buzz was her rock.

"I know you'd help," she said now. "But to be honest, I'm not entirely sure that you can help me right now."

"With this profile that you don't have?"

Elle nodded and took another drink. The woman across the bar turned and she could see a regular profile, a sharp nose. She'd leave her number with the woman before she left, she vowed. Maybe even try to buy her a drink.

"So, who's this profile supposed to be of then?" Buzz asked. "I mean, we could try and set it up real fast, call their agent or whatever. I'm sure we can work it out. It's not that big of a deal. You just told Kim before you actually got it set up, that's all."

"Oh no," Elle said, turning back to Buzz. "It's a big deal."

"Who is it then?"

She took a deep breath and wondered at her own sanity. Out of all the people in all the world, why the hell had she chosen this one? It was like for a brief second there she'd actually lost her mind. She felt shaky and nauseous just thinking about it.

"Elle, just tell me."

"Alya Goldstein." It came out as a whisper, so quiet that she was sure Buzz hadn't heard. So she said it louder, this time almost at a shout. "Alya Goldstein."

And Buzz's face turned into a palette of O's. Her eyes were round and open, her eyebrows raised, her mouth a perfect circle. Elle picked up Buzz's drink and handed it to her. Buzz took a sip, eyes still on her, and almost choked.

"Jesus," she said, when she'd recovered her breath. "Jesus, Elle. What the hell were you thinking?"

"Dunno," and she sounded sad and sheepish.

"Alya Goldstein? As in the great mystery woman? The rich entrepreneur that never does interviews. That doesn't have photo shoots. That most people couldn't even identify if they had to?"

"Yep," Elle said. Which was kind of the point. The idea wouldn't have saved her job if it had been just any old regular interview. Unfortunately, she seemed to have slid from 'soap opera star that will literally pay to be interviewed' all the way over to 'has never done an interview ever before' in the space of just one afternoon. She really needed to work on this pitching business.

"Oh Elle, what are you going to do?"

She didn't realize until just that moment that she'd been hoping for Buzz to have some idea, hoping that Buzz would somehow, magically know how to solve this problem. It was clear, however, that Buzz had precisely zero tricks up her sleeve. Crap. "Dunno," Elle said again.

Buzz took a deeper drink, composing herself. "You could say that you made a mistake," she said. "Tell Kim that it was agreed and that Goldstein pulled out."

The woman across the bar stood up and for a second looked to be heading toward the bathroom. But she swerved at the last minute and made for the exit instead. Just her luck. The woman disappeared out of her life forever.

"I could," she allowed.

She could. She could pretend that all of this was a giant mistake. A misunderstanding even. But... But that wouldn't save her job. A job that, in all honesty, desperately needed saving.

"I could," she said again. "But I'm not going to."

She took a huge drink of her Jack and Coke, the alcohol working now, making her feel better, braver, bigger. She would do this. She could do this. She'd find a way.

"You're not going to?" Buzz was looking at her like she was crazy.

"Nope," Elle said.

"So what *are* you going to do, exactly?"

"I'm going to do the interview," she said, with far more confidence than she felt.

"Um, how?"

It was on the tip of her tongue to say 'dunno' for the third time in the last five minutes. But she bit it back. She was a journalist, dammit. She was going to do her job. Journalists got stories all the time, they got interviews with hermits, with jail-birds, with all kinds of people. How hard could it really be? She just needed to work at it, that was all. Come up with a plan.

"I'll think of something," she said.

She wasn't giving herself the choice. Come hell or highwater she was getting the damn interview. She had something to prove, to Kim, to Buzz, to herself. She was a journalist and she was going to interview Alya Goldstein.

"Here," said the waitress, sliding a shot glass across to Elle. Elle raised a questioning eyebrow. "From the woman over there."

Elle looked across to see the androgynous woman she'd been eyeing all evening back in her seat and raising a glass to her. Huh. She hadn't left after all. Maybe her luck was changing.

Chapter Four

Strapping her skates on, Alya felt the familiar thrill of getting out onto the floor. The sound of wheels skating over hard wood was ringing through the arena, and already she could hear clashes as bodies connected with the ground.

"Ten laps, no contact," the coach shouted as she took her first perilous step out into the ring.

And then she felt like she was flying. Her feet took on a life of their own and she was building up speed and the ground was sliding away under her. Her breath came faster as she completed the first lap and went into the next. This, this was how she could forget everything.

Roller derby wasn't exactly the hobby she'd been looking for. If anything, she'd fallen into it. Her shrink had suggested setting aside two hours a week for something non-work related and Alya had shown up at the bookstore next door for a book club.

A book club that had been full of women who couldn't seem to look her in the eye. Yet still, she'd figured she'd go back, fulfill her responsibilities, dutifully spend two hours without thinking about work. Even if Jane Eyre did little to distract her.

Until she'd come out of the bookstore, drinking in the cool night air, and seen a bunch of women giggling and hooting, disheveled and bruised and exhausted looking. And somehow, that had been what she wanted.

It hadn't taken long to figure out that they'd been at derby practice. So Alya had signed herself up. Now, once a week, she had exactly what her therapist had recommended. A complete break from real life. Not that she was about to make the team or anything, but the practices at least kept her mind off things.

"Come on, ladies, y'all eat snails this morning, let's speed things up here!"

She put on an extra spurt of speed, straining the muscles in her thighs as she tried to get faster still.

And here, nobody knew who she was. Nobody cared. All anyone cared about was getting faster, winning, getting better, and in helmets and mouthguards it wasn't like anyone was recognizable anyway. No, here, Alya could be whoever she wanted.

"Right, we're going ten practice laps, come collect a shirt, reds versus yellows, full contact. I want to see fierceness, ladies. You two over there, you'll be jammers for this round, grab a shirt each."

She skated over, breathless, to pick up her shirt. Red. A good color. Others pushed past her. She was surrounded by toned thighs, tight backsides, lycra and sweat. And just for a second her hormones took control, just for a second she looked, wanted, and then withdrew. Sure, some of the women here were attractive. Many were gay. But, and here was the thing, they were connected to her in some way.

Not that she never had sex. She certainly did. Her needs were taken care of. There was the occasional friend with benefits. Some one night stands. But nothing serious. Ever. And she made it a rule never to indulge with anyone connected to her. 'Don't shit where you eat,' was what a long-ago mentor had told her, and she stuck closely by the rule.

So derby ladies were off the menu.

Besides, she had more important things to think about. Like not getting any of her teeth knocked out.

The whistle blew and she took off, sliding into the first open space that she found.

SHE WAS HOME BY EIGHT, showered and at her desk again by half past. She was checking through her messages when there was a knock on the door.

"Bubbale? Are you home?"

Immediately, Alya stood up. "Is everything okay?" It was unlike her grandmother to disturb her in the office.

Shoshanna shuffled in, stick at the ready, legs obviously paining her today. Alya hurried and pulled out a chair so that her grandmother could sit, which she did with a contented sigh.

"Everything's fine, Bubbale. You shouldn't worry so much. I haven't seen you all day and I wanted to see your smile, that's all."

Alya went back behind her desk and sat down. Unlikely to be true, but she knew that her grandmother couldn't help pouring on a little of the guilt when she got the chance.

"And I came to tell you that Rachel won't be here next Friday, she has to go to her nephew's wedding."

"Aha," Alya said.

Rachel was the result of her and her grandmother's most vicious argument to date. A carer that Shoshanna was adamant that she didn't need, but that Alya knew she had to have. They had fought for weeks before compromising. Rachel had joined them on a week long trial and had never left. She was indispensable during the day when Alya was working, and occasionally at night when she had to travel.

"I'll call the agency and get a temp," she said now. "Just for that one day," she added, before Shoshanna could argue.

"You look tired, little one. You should have your assistant call, delegate more."

"I would if I had an assistant." Her grandmother frowned. "She walked out last week," Alya said. "Something about my being too demanding."

"And were you?"

Alya looked into her grandmother's dark eyes and then smiled. She never could lie to her. "Probably."

"Then find a new one."

"I'm working on it, in between everything else."

Shoshanna settled back into her chair. "As for everything else, maybe it's about time you told me what was going on. Come on, I know something's been on your mind. Tell me about it and ease your burden, little one."

Alya hesitated for a moment, but then decided on spilling the truth. She valued Shoshanna's opinions, and her grandmother had more than once spotted something that she herself had missed. Shoshanna listened intently as Alya explained.

"So, you want to expand into something else, make more money there and use that money to subsidize delivery costs for MedSend," Shoshanna said, summing up neatly when Alya was done. "It seems to me that there's only one area that would really make sense to expand into."

Alya bit her lip and nodded, saying nothing, wanting to see if Shoshanna came to the same conclusions as she did.

"Drugstore deliveries," Shoshanna said. "Prescriptions and drugstores are already linked in people's minds. It makes it an easier sell."

"Exactly," said Alya. "Precisely what I thought."

"So?"

"So, I'm setting up a meeting with a man called Lars Berger. He started an app that's somewhat similar to MedSend, except it works with drugstores to deliver toiletries and other small items to customers."

"And you're looking for?"

Alya shrugged. "A buyout if possible, if he'll agree and I can get the investment money. A merger otherwise, though that's not the way I really want to go."

Shoshanna laughed. "Always so independent, little one. There's nothing wrong with merging, nothing wrong with having two heads instead of one."

"Mmm." She didn't want to argue with her grandmother, not tonight.

"You think this Berger will sell?"

"Not a clue," Alya said, honestly. "I know nothing about him. I'm doing my research and then I'll set up the meet."

Shoshanna nodded. "Good girl. And in the meantime, perhaps you have time for something else?"

"Like?"

"Like, Rachel's daughter's best friend's sister is coming to town and—"

"And she's gay?" Alya said. She took a deep breath, putting her anger to one side. Her grandmother loved her and cared for her and was trying to help. "No, Bubbe. No blind dates. No dates period."

"Sometimes it's the blind dates that end up best," Shoshanna said, pushing herself up from the chair. "It's the ones you don't know. The ones you discover. Sometimes they have happy endings."

Alya stood and went to her grandmother, taking her elbow and helping her navigate to the door. "I don't believe in happy endings," she said.

Her grandmother grunted, but said nothing. This was an argument they'd definitely had before. They walked together to the door and then Alya let go.

"I'll say good night now," Shoshanna said. "I've got the new Patricia Cornwell to take to bed, so I'll have an early night."

"Good night, Bubbe," Alya said, kissing her grandmother's soft cheek and knowing that if there were murder in the works then her grandmother wouldn't be sleeping any time soon. She was a crime addict and would read for most of the night. Alya rued the day when someone taught Shoshanna about podcasts, she'd never hear a word from her grandmother again.

"And hire yourself an assistant," Shoshanna said, shuffling down the hallway and leaning on her stick. "You need someone to help you. Besides, it doesn't look right, the chief of a company without an assistant."

"I will."

"You make sure you do!"

Alya grinned and closed the door to her office. Shoshanna wasn't wrong. She made a mental note to move hiring an assistant higher up her list of priorities.

Chapter Five

Elle reached for the remote and switched off the TV. Her hands were sticky from popcorn and her eyes were gritty from too much screen-time.

"Had your nineties thrills?" Buzz asked, passing by the living room.

Elle threw a cushion at her, which Buzz deftly caught and came in to return it to the couch.

"The Devil Wears Prada came out in 2006, and Sex and the City didn't go off air until, like, 2004 or something," she said.

"Yeah. Right. 'Cos that makes a difference. I'm pretty sure that you don't get journalistic training from watching either Miranda Priestly or Carrie Bradshaw," Buzz said, sitting on the arm of the sofa and then sliding down so that she banged onto the cushion next to Elle.

"It was inspiration," Elle said, pouting. Not bad inspiration exactly, but, well, not exactly helpful either, if she were being honest.

Buzz patted her knee. "You'll get there. Probably. Maybe. I mean, you have a degree and everything."

"Yeah, but it focussed more on proper grammar than it did on kidnapping famous people and forcing them to do interviews."

"Really? That surprises me," said Buzz. "What about blackmail or bribery, did it cover those?"

"Nope, definitely not part of the curriculum."

Buzz grinned and took Elle's hand. "You've worked harder at this than I think I've ever seen you work at anything job-related."

Elle eyed the pile of papers and her open laptop on the coffee table. It was true. She'd put her time in, done her research. She'd scoured journals and newspapers and magazines and the internet for every scrap of knowledge about Alya Goldstein. Unfortunately, what she'd found out was about enough to fill a Post-It note. Thus turning to movies and TV for some kind of inspiration.

She groaned. "I don't know, Buzz. I really don't. I'm not getting anywhere."

"You called?"

She rolled her eyes. "Obviously. But no one will speak to me and it's got to the point where anyone that picks up the phone at MedSend just hangs up on me immediately."

Buzz sighed. "Maybe you should go and explain everything to Kim."

The thought of the look in Kim's eyes, the sneer on her face, and more importantly the words that would come out of her mouth, made Elle feel sick and sweaty. There was no doubt that she'd get fired if she showed up and said that she'd lied. Which she had. She was coming to terms with the fact that she could dress this up in all the pretty words she liked and it was still lying, and sooner or later she'd be paying the consequences.

"No," she said, sitting up. "No, I'm not ready for that yet. I'm not giving in. Quitters never win and all that."

And she had something to prove and she had no other options and she didn't know what the hell she'd do if she got fired from *Edina*.

"Well, I guess you could show up in person," Buzz said doubtfully.

Elle nodded in thought. Yes, yes, that could work. Spring a surprise on her. If nothing else, maybe she could collar some of the employees at MedSend into talking. Maybe she could even talk her way in past security. Her stomach felt a little lighter. The idea was definitely growing on her.

THE FLOOR WAS WHITE and tiled, the elevators and stair rails chrome, and the only seats were horrific concoctions of black leather and silver metal that made Elle's back scream just from looking at them. But the entire front wall of the office building was glass, and light streamed in fresh and bright and maybe, just maybe, her luck was going to change today.

She felt a strange tingling over her skin, a premonition she was sure, that she was in the right place, doing the right thing. The same tingling she'd felt walking into her first journalism class. She could do this.

She walked straight up to the reception desk, where a blonde woman was filing her nails.

"Can I help you?"

Elle took a deep breath. "Yes, I'm here to see Alya Goldstein."

The woman frowned. "I'm sorry, Ms. Goldstein isn't in yet. Is she expecting you?"

The last time she'd lied had gotten her into this mess. Probably she should tell the truth now. But her mouth wouldn't form the words. Instead she came out with an "mm-hmm" which sounded like neither a yes nor a no.

The blonde huffed and pouted. "Ms. Goldstein's assistant quit last week, and we've been having problems with her schedule ever since. I'm so sorry. If you'd just take a seat over there, Ms. Goldstein should be in shortly."

She walked over to the black leather chairs, her heels loud on the tiled floor, wondering if it really could be this easy. If she could really just waltz into Goldstein's office like this. She looked around her, there was no one else. The blonde receptionist had gone back to filing her nails. She might actually be able to get away with this.

She rolled her shoulders, took deep breaths, and tried to concentrate on the questions she was going to ask. She was sure that once she was inside, in the inner sanctum, then Goldstein wouldn't be able to throw her out. Right?

Her face was flushing now. She was sure this was it. Okay, so she'd had to lie. But wasn't that just what journalists did? They did what they had to to get the story, right?

"Miss? Miss?"

It took a second before she realized that the receptionist was talking to her.

"Miss?"

"Uh, yes?" She didn't get up. It was like now that she was in her seat it was her place, she had a right to sit in it.

"Miss, I'm sorry, could you come up to the desk, please?"

Elle sucked her teeth, but it wasn't like she had much choice. Still though, she really didn't want to get up. Reluctantly, she stood, straightening her skirt, tucking in her blouse, taking her time before slowly, slowly walking over to the desk.

"Is there a problem?" she asked as casually as she could.

The blonde smiled. "I'm an idiot, I didn't even ask for your name. I'm sorry, it's just... I'm not a morning person, you know?"

"Tell me about it," Elle said, leaning in. "I can't even speak until I've had at least two coffees."

The blonde grinned. "My boyfriend just doesn't get that at all. He's always trying to talk to me in the mornings, like, I keep telling him to just keep schtum until I've had some caffeine, but does he listen? Honestly, men."

"Men," Elle echoed, raising her eyes to the ceiling and praying to any kind of God that the blonde was about to forget about taking her details. "Can't live with them."

"Not allowed to kill them," the blonde laughed.

Elle laughed too, feeling the ice breaking, feeling like she was getting somewhere. Until the blonde spoke again.

"So, yeah, I just need to see some ID please."

Elle blew out a breath. One glimpse of her ID and the game was up. She'd called the building enough times now that there's no way her name wouldn't be recognized. "I, um, left it in my car?"

The blonde frowned. "Really? But you have your purse right there."

"Oh, oh," Elle pretended to be shocked, then embarrassed, not exactly hard to do. "So I do. Yeah. Well, the thing is that, um, my ID was stolen. Just a couple of nights ago actually, you know that new bar down on ninth street? It was there. Great place, by the way, great drinks."

But the blonde wasn't buying it, wasn't about to be distracted again. "I'm afraid I do need to see some ID." Her tone was harder now, her eyes narrowing.

"I told you, I don't have any."

"Then I have to ask you to leave."

Elle glanced around, anxiously looking for something, anything that might help her. And just as her eyes were sweeping over the door, it opened.

A tall woman walked in, short dark hair slicked back, high heels leading up to slim legs encased in ankle-length pants, her stride long and forceful and strong. Elle didn't even need to see her face to know that this was Alya Goldstein.

Her eyes lingered over her body, lithe, androgynous. Her heart beat a little harder as she glimpsed a hint of cleavage in the V of the white shirt Goldstein was wearing. And by the time her eyes had crawled up to the face, to the long, aquiline nose, the olive skin, the green, cat-like eyes, her palms were sweating and her mouth was dry.

Fuck.

She hadn't realized Goldstein was a knock-out. A pulse pounded between her legs. And she forgot everything except drooling over the woman in front of her.

"Ms. Goldstein?" the receptionist was saying.

The dark woman stopped, her eyebrows raised in impatience. "Yes?"

"This woman is here to see you, but—"

"About damn time," Goldstein snapped. She looked Elle up and down. "Follow me."

She strode off, leaving Elle bewildered and the receptionist staring after her.

"But she's got no ID," the receptionist cried.

"She's with me," said Goldstein, mashing the button of the elevator and not turning round.

Elle could barely breathe. She didn't dare look at the receptionist as she hesitantly began to walk toward the elevator. Then the doors slid open and she hurried.

She had no idea what she was doing, but whatever the hell had just happened had been in her favor.

She'd just have to figure out the details as she went along.

Chapter Six

From the side of her eye, Alya examined the woman standing next to her in the elevator.

Mid-length blonde hair. It didn't look dyed, she thought. Regular features, skin slightly pale, eyes deep blue with long, black lashes. Definitely make-up there, but not plastered on, just a touch. She allowed herself to look lower. Dark suit, pale blouse, rounded hips and breasts, a skirt with shapely legs revealed, and high heels.

Decent enough, she thought. Normal looking, nothing special. But her look would fit with the company's. Not that looks were everything, of course they weren't. But then just yesterday she'd interviewed a woman with a mohawk. Not exactly the professional kind of impression she was looking to make.

So, all in all, the present candidate was doing well so far. She hadn't opened her mouth though. Which was both good and bad. Good in that she was comfortable with silence and hadn't said anything stupid yet. Bad in that it could show lack of confidence.

The elevator stopped and the doors opened. Alya strode out.

"Follow me," she said, without looking back to see if she was indeed being followed.

ELLE WASN'T STUPID. It was obvious that there was some kind of misunderstanding going on here. And to be honest, she didn't particularly care what it was. As long as she got inside Alya Goldstein's office and got at least the beginnings of a story, she'd be happy. She was perfectly willing to play along for now. She'd choose her moment carefully.

It was like being undercover, she thought to herself with a pleasant thrill.

She let herself be led towards large, double doors, and then through them into an office outfitted in white and pine, soothing and quiet. So this was the inner sanctum, was it? She was already starting to compose an introduction to her profile in her head.

"Take a seat, please," Goldstein said.

Elle did as she was told while Goldstein went behind her desk. She kept quiet, folding her hands in her lap, wanting to see where this was going to go. Goldstein's green eyes watched her until her insides were squirming. Those lips did look very kissable.

"So, tell me why you want to work for MedSend."

Aha. Her first clue. Goldstein thought she was a job candidate, did she? Okay, Elle could work with that. She'd done enough damn research on the company.

"Well, I think I'd be a great fit," she began.

VERY LITTLE ESCAPED Alya's attention. She was detail oriented, always had been. And there was something off about the woman in front of her. She couldn't quite put her finger on it. She'd assumed nerves at first, assumed that the woman wasn't prepared for the interview.

But once she started to speak, she was clear and concise, confident, and obviously knew more than enough about MedSend.

"I think giving back is important, helping those less fortunate than ourselves is important, and most of all, making the world a better place is important, just a little at a time," the woman was saying. Her smile showed even white teeth.

"I see." Alya opened up her computer, searching through her agenda, looking for the woman's CV and name. She was damned if she could remember the name. The hiring agency had definitely told her, she must have written it somewhere.

But she did notice that the woman's eyes were wandering around her office the second she thought that Alya wasn't paying attention to her.

Taking an angry breath in, Alya admitted defeat. "I'm so sorry," she said. "Things haven't been running smoothly here, which rather obviously is why I need to hire a new assistant. Do you happen to have a copy of your CV with you?"

The woman's eyes widened for a second and Alya almost thought she could see fear.

IT DIDN'T TAKE A GENIUS to put the pieces together. Or to see the potential here. Elle's mind whirled. She was very obviously being interviewed for the position of Alya Goldstein's assistant. In a millisecond her mind had torn through all the possibilities that that offered.

Screw a profile interview.

This really was being undercover.

If she wanted to write a true profile, real journalism, then this could be her chance, couldn't it?

Her heart was beating harder and she felt a drip of sweat roll down her spine. She could tell the truth right now. Right this second, she could end this. She could do the right thing. The honorable thing.

Or she could keep up the pretense.

Her teeth itched with indecision.

"My CV?" she asked, playing for time.

"Mmm, I must have misplaced it," Goldstein said, scrolling through something on her screen. She turned to Elle and those green eyes burned into her and suddenly there was a smile so bright it warmed Elle's bones. The eyes danced, a dimple appeared in her right cheek. "I'm afraid I don't even remember your name."

She could tell the truth now.

Or she could get the story.

Her heart beat even harder.

She needed to tread carefully.

"EXACTLY THE KIND OF thing that wouldn't happen if I were your assistant," the woman said archly.

Alya cocked an eyebrow. There was a confidence there that hadn't been there a moment ago. Almost like the woman had decided on something, decided she wanted the job perhaps. "How so?"

"I'm extremely organized," the woman said. "Nothing would be lost on my watch. I'm also efficient, I have a high typing speed, I'm personable and very used to working with the public."

All the qualities she was looking for really. But still, there was something not quite right. "And your CV?"

The woman sniffed. "I'm afraid I don't have a copy on me just now, I assumed you already had one. But I'm happy to email one to you as soon as possible."

Alya reached for the stack of business cards on her desk only to find that the box was empty. Christ, she really needed an assistant. She opened a drawer, then another, until finally she found a card. "Here, please email that to me directly."

"Of course," the woman said. She paused, looked down like she was thinking, then back up again. "I, uh, I hope you don't mind me saying this, but I want this job. I'm prepared to work hard, prepared to work odd hours, anything you ask of me. You're an inspiration to me, and the work you do is so important."

Nice to hear, particularly since her last assistant had thought that she was too demanding. Alya nodded. "I see."

"I'm well-qualified, as you'll see when you get my CV. And, and, well, I'm very discrete. That's obviously a key quality in a personal assistant."

The key quality as far as Alya was concerned. She nodded again, then smiled. "I'm glad to hear that. Do you have any questions about the company?"

The woman shook her head. "No, thank you."

The answer didn't surprise Alya. The woman sounded like she knew what she was talking about, like she'd taken the time to learn about the company before interviewing. Always a good sign.

Something was stopping her from pulling the trigger though. She wasn't sure what. Maybe she just needed a little time to think about things. Normally she was so decisive.

"Very well, I'll get back to you in the next few days," she said, worried now at her own lack of decisiveness. She needed an assistant. This woman sounded perfect, and yet...

"Of course, thank you so much for your time."

The woman stood up, offered her hand, and Alya took it. The hand was smaller than her own, warm, soft. But the handshake didn't linger. The woman smiled, a bright smile that crinkled in the corner of her eyes and Alya suddenly noticed that her breasts swelled to fill her shirt rather nicely. She tore her eyes away and looked into the woman's face. They shared a smile, and then she turned to go.

She made it all the way to the door before Alya stopped her.

"Uh, sorry."

The woman turned, that almost fearful look in her eyes again. "Yes?"

"Sorry," Alya said, embarrassed at having forgotten. What had gotten into her this morning? "Sorry, but your name?"

"Elle."

She noted it down on a piece of paper, not trusting herself just now to remember anything. A pretty name. Short but sweet. Easy to remember. It suited her, she thought. A soft, sweet name for a sweet, innocent looking face like that. "Um, Elle what?" she asked.

She wasn't looking up, her pen poised over the paper, so she could have misjudged things, could have been mistaken. But she could have sworn that there was just the hint of a hesitation before the woman replied.

"Smith. Elle Smith."

Alya looked up, but the woman was already walking away, the door already closing behind her. Weird. The perfect candidate. Probably. So why was she so hesitant?

"I need coffee," she said out loud.

She reached out for the buzzer by her desk, before realizing that there was no assistant to bring her caffeine.

"Shit."

She stared at the door. She could call the woman back. Or she could play safe and interview another couple of candidates.

She sighed and got up. She'd make her own coffee. Playing safe seemed like the smart thing to do.

Chapter Seven

Back in the office she still couldn't quite believe it. No, strike that, she didn't believe it at all. Any minute now she was going to get busted, though if she took more than a second to think about it she couldn't figure out how. After all, she'd never left her name anywhere, so how could anyone at MedSend know who she was?

Which didn't stop her stomach aching with fear and excitement every time she thought about what she'd just done.

She grabbed her purse, stuffed her phone into it and walked away from her desk. She couldn't concentrate anyway, there was no point in her being here.

"Elle!"

She'd just about made it to the door when Kim's voice stopped her. She groaned, painted on a smile, and turned back.

"Yes?" she asked, a picture of innocence.

Kim pursed her lips and narrowed her eyes so that Elle felt herself under inspection. "How's the Goldstein story going?"

Hurriedly, Elle slipped into the office, closing the door behind her. She wanted to keep this secret for a million reasons, not least because she didn't want the humiliation of failing in front of the entire office.

"It's going well," she said, as non-committally as possible.

"Mm-hmm. And?"

"And, um, I'm working on it."

Kim breathed in deeply through her nose, trying, Elle thought, to hold on to her patience. "Forgive me, Elle, but I really do think you should try and see things from my point of view here."

"Which is?"

"Which is that you, far from my strongest team member, are telling me that you've got a profile of one of the hottest, most mysterious, most notoriously private women in the world. And I'm supposed to just trust you on all of this?"

Elle bit her lip, swallowed, then nodded.

"Seriously?"

A flash of irritation burst in front of her eyes. She hated not being believed. The fact that she'd lied to Kim was by the by. She actually was, kind of, telling the truth now, wasn't she?

She put her hands on Kim's desk. "This morning I was in Alya Goldstein's private office," she said. "Sitting as close to her as you are to me now."

Kim's mouth opened, but then she closed it. And nodded. "Alright, alright."

Elle stood up. "I'm working on something," she said. "I'll give you more details in a couple of days. Promise."

A job. The job. Going undercover. She felt that thrill again. Okay, it was mostly luck, but if she got the assistant job...

"Fine, fine," Kim said. Elle was half-way to the door before Kim's voice stopped her again. "Don't make me regret this, Baker."

"I won't," Elle said, unable to look her in the eye.

She really, really hoped that she wouldn't.

BUZZ SCREECHED LOUDLY enough that the bartender spun around and stared at her.

"Sorry, sorry," she said, waving him away before turning back to Elle. "So, what, you just... Walked into her office?"

"I followed her into her office," Elle corrected. "Because she thought that I was a job candidate."

"Uh-huh," said Buzz. "And... And what? You interviewed for the job?"

"Yes," Elle said, aware now that it sounded crazy. "I did. It just sort of happened and I went with it. I kept thinking—"

"That it'd be like 21 Jump Street or something," finished Buzz.

Elle laughed. "See, you make fun of me for being on a nineties kick and then you go seriously old school like that. But yeah, it just occurred to me that if I could get the job then, well, I'd be in the best position to get the story too, right?"

"And if you don't get the job?"

Elle shrugged. The truth was that she didn't have a plan B. "I guess I'll start writing with what I've got. I mean, at least I've been inside her office, which is more than any other journalist has. So, I guess I get an advantage there."

"If you're writing about her décor, yeah, I guess so," Buzz said, with an eye roll. "So, what's she like?"

"Goldstein?"

"No, the Queen. Yes, Goldstein."

"Uh, she's fine." Elle's brain was reliving the interview, was reliving the moment that Alya Goldstein had walked through that door, the length of her legs, the curve of her waist, those green, green eyes.

"Fine? I'm gonna need more than that, Elle. She's like, I don't know, a hermit or something. I wanna know what she's really like. Come on, you're going to be profiling her, you're going to need to be a bit more in depth than 'she's fine.'"

Elle sighed and drank to give herself time to think. A non-alcoholic cocktail. Fizzy and fruity and not at all what she wanted to be drinking, but she had sworn off alcohol for at least two days. Though now that she was thinking about it, a foray into Alya Goldstein's office probably deserved a drink.

"She's... I don't know. Cold, like there's a barrier there, something she doesn't let people behind, which is understandable I guess. Smart, definitely, observant. She seemed…" She blew out a breath and shook her head. "I don't know, I need more time with her. I spent about seven minutes with her."

Seven minutes and yes, Goldstein had been kind of unapproachable and cold, but then, Elle thought, perhaps she was also lonely. She didn't seem like she'd been surrounded by friends and family. What little she knew about the woman suggested that she was a loner. And maybe, just maybe, there was something a little warmer behind that wall she was putting up. A wall that Elle was going to have to breach if there was going to be any kind of decent story here.

"Right…" Buzz said. "And? No, wait, don't tell me." Buzz peered in closer, then laughed. "She was attractive, wasn't she? You're blushing. You always do this when you talk about a woman you like. You clam up and can barely even describe her. Elle!"

"No!" Elle said, sitting up straighter. "Nothing like that!" She gave up and pushed her drink away, gesturing to the bartender to give her a martini like the one Buzz was drinking. Just one drink.

"Then what?"

Elle sighed. "Okay, she's attractive. Very attractive actually." With that severe dark hair and that dimple when she smiled. Elle's stomach flipped. "But she's also a rich bitch."

"Aha, I forgot about that."

"About what?" Elle asked, gratefully accepting the martini.

"About your prejudice against anyone that earns more than a basic salary," Buzz said. "And, just for the record, she might be rich, but you've got no idea if she's a rich bitch, since by your own admission she spent no more than seven minutes with her."

"She owns a company. Money will be more important than people. She's a rich bitch. I guarantee it." The martini tasted like heaven. "Trust me, Buzz. I know her type. I grew up with them, after all."

Buzz looked like she was going to say something, but Elle stared at her and she changed her mind. Which was a good thing. Elle really didn't want to fight with Buzz today. Not after the weird kind of day she'd had.

"So, you're really going to try and get this job?" Buzz asked.

Elle nodded. "I faked a CV and sent it to her this afternoon." She'd gone as far as to go out to an old internet cafe and send the CV from there, just in case Goldstein had anyone smart enough to track where her emails were coming from. The last thing she needed was for an email to give her away.

In fact, she'd almost given herself away, titling the entire CV with her real name, Elle Baker, before realizing her mistake at the last minute and changing it to Elle Smith. Not her most creative of moments, she had to admit. But at least the name sounded real, and hopefully was common enough that an internet search would bring up tons of results and obscure the fact that her face wasn't among them.

Buzz held up her glass. "I gotta hand it to you, Elle. I was wrong. I said that maybe journalism wasn't for you. And now you've gone and gotten all Watergate and stuff on me. I'm impressed."

"Watergate was a cover-up for... Oh, never mind," Elle said, raising her own glass. "To being undercover."

"To getting undercover," said Buzz pointedly. "You haven't got the job yet."

Elle drank deeply. She couldn't think about that. Getting the job was the only thread she had to cling onto at the moment. Without it, she had no clue what she was going to do. End up homeless and living in a box, probably. The alcohol burned her throat. Her fate was in someone else's hands, never a good position to be in.

"I'll get the job," she said.

But she wasn't quite as confident as she sounded.

Chapter Eight

Alya looked across at the girl. Girl was the right word. She looked young. She also looked like she was about to cry.

"Is there anything else you can tell me about yourself?" she asked, patiently.

The girl just shook her head and kept looking down at her hands.

Alya was very careful to place to CV down on her desk gently, careful not to show any sign of irritation. She had a feeling that the girl would weep at the drop of a hat and that was really the last thing that she needed.

"Thank you very much for coming in. I'll let you know in a couple of days," she said.

The girl sat silently for a second and Alya became increasingly worried that she was going to have to get security to escort her out. But finally, she stood, and exited without a word.

Alya sat back in her chair and sighed. Surprisingly, this had not been the worst candidate for the job. Nor had the mohawk girl. Yesterday afternoon there had been a male assistant that had called her 'honey' twice during his interview, and another woman that had insisted that since she had small children she could only work until three.

All in all, there was really only one decent candidate in the lot. Elle Smith.

But there was still something niggling there, still something that had seemed off.

There were a dozen reasons to hire the girl, not least her efficiency and the fact that Elle could look her in the eye. Not hiring her because she gave off a strange vibe seemed... wrong somehow.

Not hiring her because she was attractive, now that had to be some kind of discrimination. Not that Alya hired on looks, she didn't, really didn't. But it wasn't looks exactly. There had been something about Elle, the way she moved, the gleam in her eye, that in another time and another place would have made Alya interested.

Interested in a one night stand, of course, nothing more.

Because there were no relationships, no happy ending. She wasn't a child, she didn't believe in fairytales.

Her phone rang.

"Alya Goldstein."

"Oh." There was a pause and then someone cleared their throat. Someone that had obviously been expecting to go through at least one assistant before getting Alya on the phone. "Um, yes, I'm from Fortune Magazine, I'm looking for—"

"Nope," Alya said.

"I just need—"

"No," said Alya firmly. "No interviews, no quotes, no pictures. Thank you. Bye now."

She hung up.

This was why she needed an assistant. She needed a gate-keeper, an organizer, someone who... who could help her take care of her life.

Because sometimes, just sometimes, her life seemed too big and complicated to take care of all by herself.

She knew what her grandmother would say about that. She needed a girlfriend, preferably a wife, to help her take care of things. Not a route she was willing to take. She'd decided long ago that the single life was for her. Six years old, lying in her bed at night listening to the crash of china and the buzz of raised voices below, she'd known that a calm life, a quiet life, had to be solely her own.

A list of priorities was squared in the corner of her desk. She had a finite amount of time and too many things to fill it. Definitely not enough time to be thinking about the past, which certainly wasn't something that deserved thinking about.

She picked up her phone, dialed a number, was connected after the first ring.

"Lars Berger's office."

So he had an assistant then. Hardly surprising. Alya wondered idly if she could poach the woman, offer her more money, get her over here this afternoon, be done with the whole ordeal of trying to hire someone new.

"Lars Berger's office," said the impatient voice again.

"Yes, this is Alya Goldstein, I'd like to set up an appointment with Mr. Berger."

There was a slight pause as fingers clicked over a keyboard, then the voice came back. "We'll call you back with the details. Thank you for calling."

And Alya was left holding a disconnected call. She stared at the phone in her hand for a second. The assistant had obviously thought that she was an assistant too, despite the fact that she'd given her own name. Hardly an auspicious start to what she was hoping was going to be a very profitable arrangement.

And yet another reason why she just needed to damn well hire someone. Why was she being so indecisive about this?

The phone rang.

"Alya—"

"Mr. Berger has a slot on Thursday at ten fifteen, I'll pencil Ms. Goldstein in."

"Tha—"

But the phone had already been hung up again. There was something about that kind of ruthless efficiency that Alya liked. Maybe she could poach the woman. If she hadn't found a new assistant by the time she went over there, she may just take her chances and give it a try...

SOMEHOW HER GRANDMOTHER'S apartment always managed to smell like chicken soup. It was a comforting smell, a childhood smell, and one that made Alya smile when she walked through the door.

"I'm in and out, Bubbe," she said.

"And aren't you looking fabulous?" Shoshanna smiled.

"I've got a business dinner," Alya said, looking down at the dress she was wearing. "You don't think this is too much?"

"No, not at all. It's nice to see you in a dress for a change. You look lovely. Very... feminine."

"Grandma..."

Shoshanna held up both hands. "Okay, okay." She smiled again. "And who else will be at this dinner? Anyone important? Someone special perhaps?"

Alya sat down on the ottoman. "If you keep insinuating things then I'll stop telling you where I'm going and when," she said.

Shoshanna sighed. "Fine, fine. I should stop. I can't help it though. I think it's a grandmother thing. From the moment you were born I just had all this extra worry and sometimes it escapes my mouth."

"How are you feeling today?" asked Alya, changing the subject. "Meds good? Blood sugar okay? Did Rachel leave any notes for me?"

"I do wish the two of you wouldn't have all this secret communication, like I'm a child or something. And no, she left you nothing. Everything is fine. I took my medicines like a good girl and my blood sugars have been fine all day."

Alya nodded. "I should be going then. Don't wait up, I'll probably be late."

"There is one thing," Shoshanna said as Alya stood up.

"Mmm?" She was distracted by taking out her phone, ready to call for the town car to come and collect her.

"Ruth called."

Alya stopped in her tracks, frozen for a brief moment in time. When she realized that she wasn't moving she deliberately went back to her phone, not looking at her grandmother, not showing anything out of the ordinary. "She did?" she said, as though the news was of zero interest to her.

Shoshanna sighed. "Alya, Bubbale, it would be nice if you could call her back."

"I'm very busy." And if she weren't busy she could definitely make herself busy in order to avoid the call.

"She's your mother."

"It's not like I could forget."

It was like a switch had been thrown. One mention of her mother's name and suddenly Alya had become a sullen teenager again. She hated herself for it, and hated that her mother could still have such an effect on her.

"Alya Goldstein, you're not too old to be put over my knee."

Alya glanced at her grandmother and saw that she was half-serious. "Fine, I deserved that. I'm sorry."

"You should call your mother."

Her inability to lie to her grandmother wasn't always particularly convenient. In the end she settled for a nod, which in her head meant 'yes, of course, I'll consider the idea' but which to her grandmother almost certainly signaled 'yes, of course I'll call my mother.' It was the best she could do.

"Go on, Bubbale, be safe and have a nice time."

Alya kissed her grandmother and left.

There were too many people in her world, she thought, as she waited for the silent elevator to arrive on her floor. Too many people who needed to talk to her, who wanted things from her. Given her own way she thought that she could quite happily hole up in her apartment with her grandmother and never deal face to face with anyone ever again.

Maybe that was her life goal. To become some sort of weird Howard Hughes recluse. That way she wouldn't need to meet anyone or talk to anyone or interview anyone or anything else.

She stepped into the elevator when the doors opened, feet sinking into thick carpet. Expensive carpet. She wasn't quite as rich as Howard Hughes, but she was getting there. Some sound business decisions, some good investments, all were helping. And she'd had a good start in life, of course. Not quite rich enough to lock herself away from the world though.

She hit the button for the foyer.

And she still hadn't hired a damn assistant.

Chapter Nine

It had been too long. Three days since the interview. She didn't have the job. The first day she'd been excited. The second day, realistic. But now, on day three, Elle was sitting in front of her computer at work trying to reconcile herself to the fact that her lucky break hadn't been a break at all.

What the hell was she going to do?

Her stomach had shrunk to the size of a stone and her shoulders ached with the tension of it all. She needed a new plan, a new way to get at Goldstein. But she was damned if she could think of anything. She could try and get her at home, she guessed. That seemed pretty damn stalker-y though and even Elle had a line to draw somewhere.

Her mobile buzzed on her desk.

"Yes?"

Never answer the phone with your full name, a trick she'd learned very early on in working for newspapers. A journalist should give out as little information about themselves as possible.

"Is that Elle Smith?"

She almost, almost corrected her, almost gave her real name, before her brain jolted into sync with the conversation. "Yes, it is," she said as calmly as she could.

"I'd like to offer you the job that you interviewed for at MedSend."

Her heartbeat tripled, quadrupled, to the point where she was afraid to stand up in case she passed out. She squeezed her legs tight together trying to contain herself. "Oh, that's wonderful," she managed to say.

"I assume from that that you'll be taking the job?"

"Yes, absolutely, yes!"

"Perfect. If you could come in and sign a contract with HR, we'll get you on-boarded. Is this afternoon alright with you? We'd like you to start as soon as possible."

"Yes, yes, no problem at all. I'll be there as soon as I can."

She waited for a half-second after the call ended before letting out a whoop that stilled the entire office.

"Sorry, sorry!" she said as a range of disturbed faces looked at her. "Sorry!" She got up and practically ran to Kim's office.

"Was that you making that horrific noise?"

Elle could barely get the door closed, her hands were shaking and she didn't know what to do with herself. She nodded frantically, trying to decide just what to say and how to say it.

"Sit the hell down, Baker, and tell me what's going on."

She took a seat, took a breath, tried to calm herself. Then she just blurted it right out. "I just got a job as Alya Goldstein's personal assistant."

Kim's mouth dropped open and for a long second the two women stared at each other until Kim finally came to her senses. "Her assistant?"

"Yep. Legit. I can go and sign a contract with HR this afternoon. I'm in, Kim. I'm as close as I can get to Goldstein."

"This was your plan?"

Elle coughed. "Um, it was *a* plan."

Kim leaned back in her chair, crossing her legs and regarding Elle with grey eyes. "You know, Baker, I might just have underestimated you."

For the first time it occurred to Elle that she probably needed some kind of permission for this, that she should probably have run the hare-brained scheme past her editor at some point. "So it's okay then?" she asked now. "Going undercover, all that jazz?"

Kim narrowed her eyes and then nodded. "Ordinarily, I'd say no. We're not a big newspaper with a string of investigative reporters. But for this particular story, I don't see that we have much choice. I assume you went through all the normal channels?"

"Goldstein wouldn't talk to me, I never even got through to her on the phone. And no one else would either, for that matter."

Kim scratched her nose. "Alright, alright. But there need to be some ground-rules. Foremost of which is that you keep your journalistic objectivity."

"Right, got it. Be objective."

"And that you stay on the right side of the law. We've got a whole legal department here, so if you're in doubt you run things by them."

"Absolutely."

Kim tapped her fingers on the desk. "And that you're careful. Careful not to be unmasked, we don't want bad press for the magazine. Once the story's actually out, that's a different matter. But for the time being, this stays between you and I. I'll tell the rest of the team that you're off sick. You can report in by phone, but you don't need to show your face at the office."

Elle's heart was tap-dancing. She was really doing this, it was really going to happen.

"So, what are you waiting for?" Kim said. "Go on. Sign that contract. Get the story."

THE SAME BLONDE RECEPTIONIST was at the desk but this time, she greeted Elle with a smile.

"So you got the job then?" she asked.

Elle nodded.

"I'm Julia," she said, holding out her hand to shake. Elle took it. "And if you hold on for just one second, I'll get someone to come and escort you through to HR. That's where you're going, right?"

"Sure is."

Julia picked up the phone and Elle took a second to look around at the foyer. It was still bright and light, it was still open and spacious. But now it was starting to look a little more familiar. This was going to be her workplace, at least for the next couple of weeks. It couldn't take much longer than that, surely?

She'd given little thought into just how she was going to get information. For a start, just being close to Goldstein was a good thing. She'd get a sense of her personality, of how she acted, who she really was. Even if Goldstein refused to comment on anything, and she almost certainly would refuse, a profile about her would be enough. Enough, and more than anyone else had ever gotten.

How had she ended up here? It was like a miracle. Close to being fired one moment, a real, live, undercover reporter the next. It was breath-taking if she took any time to think about it at all.

"Elle Smith?" said a voice.

She turned and a dark-haired man was waiting for her.

"If you'd just follow me," he said with a wide smile.

SHE WAS SITTING IN an office with a window looking out onto a corridor, barely listening as someone explained her benefits to her. Instead, she was watching, taking in the ambiance.

MedSend seemed like a decent workplace. People didn't look stressed from what she could see. The workforce seemed predominantly young, but that wasn't unusual for a start-up. They dressed casually and looked happy.

"We'll need your details from your last insurer, as well as your social security card and all that other kind of good stuff," the man said now.

Elle nodded. She'd been prepared for this, had actually given it thought. "Not a problem. I'm just in the middle of moving though, so it might take me a few days to get all that to you."

The man smiled. "Sure, that's fine. Ms. Goldstein has asked me to speed up the hiring process and get you to work. But as long as you bring all your documentation by the end of the month, that should be fine. Make sure you do though, or else you won't get paid!"

Elle smiled automatically. And a figure strode by the window. Tall and dark and lithe and definitely Alya Goldstein.

Elle's heart skipped a beat.

Was she really doing this?

Could she really do this?

It was lying, cheating, acting, pretending. All for the sake of a story. A story that the subject didn't want released. Not exactly the most moral of decisions.

"So, if you could just sign your name here on the dotted line, you'll be officially employed."

A piece of paper was slid her way. Elle tore her eyes away from the window.

This was it. Now or never.

She could walk out now and not look back, she could extricate herself from the situation. She'd get fired, sure, but she wouldn't have to lie anymore either. And then she could... what? Work at the drive-in? Start selling her body on the corner of her street?

And suddenly in the back of her mind she could hear her father's voice, strong and hard and angry telling her that she couldn't do this. Telling her that journalism was a foolish choice. Telling her that she wasn't cut out for this lifestyle. Telling her that she was a stupid little girl who didn't know her own mind.

Yes, she could back out now. But if she did, would she ever be able to face herself in the mirror again? She doubted it.

With a shaking hand she picked up the offered pen.

Last chance, her heartbeat said, last chance to go, last chance to run. Her legs screamed at her to let them run away, her mouth dried up, she was sweating so badly that the pen almost slipped through her fingers.

Last chance for the stupid little girl who doesn't know her own mind to run away.

She pulled the contract closer and with a hurried flourish signed Elle Smith's name on the dotted line.

Chapter Ten

The office was designed to impress, and just because of that, it kind of didn't. Alya was no stranger to expensive things, and Lars Berger's office was full of them, from the art on the walls to the rug under his desk. Add to that the fact that he was making her wait and she was getting less and less impressed by the second.

She tapped her foot on the expensive rug and checked her watch. Five minutes late. A power play, obviously, and not a particularly subtle one.

Berger was a dabbler. He had his finger in pies across the city and though she was unimpressed by his office, Alya knew better than to underestimate the man. He'd made his fortune by making smart decisions. Which meant that she needed to persuade him that doing business with her was going to be a smart decision.

"Alya, Alya, so sorry to have kept you waiting."

He swept into the room, stirring a tornado of papers on his desk, and using her first name like they were already friends. As far as Alya knew, they'd never actually met before. She considered not standing up, letting him hover, embarrassed, but in the end decided that she'd better play nice. She stood and allowed him to sweep down, kissing her on both cheeks.

"So, to what do I owe the honor here?"

He rounded his desk, sank into a chair made of the softest leather, clasped his hands together. He was well dressed, his suit cut to fit him, but even the best tailoring couldn't hide a paunch and a double chin. Too much fine living. Lars Berger obviously enjoyed reaping the fruits of his labors.

She'd thought about this. Thought about playing the game, keeping secrets, holding back information. But had come to the conclusion that honesty was going to be the best policy with Berger. He was too smart to play with.

"DSD," she said.

As she'd suspected, he caught on immediately. He sucked his teeth and nodded. "Makes sense," he said. "What are we talking here?"

"A buy out."

Something else she'd put thought into. DSD ostensibly stood for Drug Store Delivery, a middlingly successful app owned by one of Berger's subsidiary companies. She could have gone to the company itself, but had decided that taking the bull by the horns was a better approach. She'd need to negotiate with Berger at some point, so why not now?

"A buy out," he echoed.

It wasn't the only possibility. It was the possibility she wanted, however. She'd prefer not to concede any kind of control to anyone else if she could help it. Besides, asking for the big prize was the best place to start a negotiation. They could always compromise later.

"We're both busy people, Mr. Berger."

"Please, call me Lars."

She smiled thinly. "We're both busy people, Lars. So you'll get no bullshitting from me. I'm interested in DSD, the full package, if it's the right price. I've done my research, I know that app downloads have been stagnating and profits are relatively stable. Your user base isn't growing, so we're not talking about an up and coming app here."

He grunted.

"And I'm sure you know a lot more about me than you're letting on. You're well aware of what would be considered a fair price for that particular slice of pie. So let's get down to brass tacks. How much?"

He sniffed, narrowed his eyes, then nodded. He pulled out a slip of paper, scribbled something on it, then slid it across the desk.

Heart in her mouth, Alya picked up the paper. The number on it was eye-wateringly high. Inside she was jumping up and down. There was no way she would or could pay the amount Berger was asking for. But the very fact that he'd given her an amount was a sign that he was willing to play ball.

She folded the paper carefully and laid it down on the desk.

"Thank you for your time," she said sweetly, before getting up to leave.

She could hear Berger's laugh as she strode down the corridor from his office. And she smiled. The game was on.

SHE WAS STILL BUZZING as she decided to hop out of the cab and walk the rest of the way to the office. It was only a couple of blocks, and traffic was all snarled up anyway. Besides, she needed time to think.

There was no way she was paying what Berger was asking. But he knew that as well as she did. She'd come up with a counter-offer in her own sweet time. An offer that Berger would think laughable, provoking him to make another counter-offer, and so on. Hopefully, they'd get to a similar price.

Whatever that price was, however, she was going to need more investment. That wasn't necessarily the worst news. She'd applied for and received investment before. In fact, her two major investors were going to be her first stop this afternoon. As much as she didn't like begging for money, it was a necessity.

She walked into the office, nodded at the receptionist, and pressed the button for the elevator. Her stomach ached at the thought of risking all she had to expand, but it was the smart choice, she knew that.

She was still thinking about how she was going to broach the subject of further investment when the elevator doors opened up into her office.

"Welcome, Ms. Goldstein, can I get a coffee for you?"

For a second she froze.

Wavy blonde hair highlighted by the sun, smooth, creamy skin, a dress that skimmed every curve and legs made longer and slimmer by high heels, there was a vision standing on the rug in front of her. A vision that made Alya's heart double-time and sent a thrill tickling over her skin.

"Ms. Goldstein?"

She had to take a breath before she could speak. This was not good, not good at all. She'd screwed up, she knew that immediately. Hiring someone that took her breath away was bad. Dangerous. Stupid.

"Uh, yes?"

"A coffee?"

She nodded briskly. "Bring it to my office."

And she walked away, through the door into her private office, before the woman could say any more.

Shit.

It had been a long time since a woman had had that effect on her. A long time since she'd had such a gut, visceral attraction to someone. She'd found the woman pretty at her interview, attractive even, but it had been different. This, the unexpected appearance of someone, had taken her by surprise and she hated herself for it.

Really, she should be able to control herself better.

She would control herself better.

It wasn't like she was a teenager with wild hormones.

A knock at the door.

"Yes?"

"Uh, Ms. Goldstein, I'm afraid that I don't know how you take your coffee. Your last assistant didn't leave any notes."

"Black," Alya said. "No sugar."

The woman nodded and Alya felt that she'd been rude, that she should be behaving better here. She cleared her throat. "You, uh, you have everything else you need? Passwords and so on?"

"HR got me all set up," the woman smiled.

The effect was less now, Alya assumed because it was no longer unexpected. But the smile still gave her goosebumps. "Coffee then."

The woman nodded and went out.

The coffee, when it came, was perfect. It tasted even better because Alya hadn't had to get up and make it herself. She'd missed having an assistant, missed being able to delegate the little things to someone else. She took a minute to quietly sip at her coffee, computer off, the office silent.

She had been rude, she realized. And it wasn't fair. After all, the woman couldn't help being attractive. This was Alya's problem, not hers. Whatever her name was. She growled under her breath, frustrated at her inability to remember.

Something short. Anne perhaps?

She took a breath, blew it out. The morning had started well. All signs from Berger were good. And then this. She'd been unfair, unfair and blunt and... And if she were truthful, she really needed the assistant. She couldn't afford to waste time hiring someone else, and she hadn't even given this one a chance yet.

She'd try harder.

And she'd start by learning the woman's name and welcoming her to the company. She stood up, determined now to be better, to be nicer. To be fairer. And not to let some stupid hormone level dictate how she was going to react to something.

Walking across the carpet, she opened up the door and for a second didn't see anyone at all. Then she heard a soft rustling and caught the scent of floral perfume. She peered around, and finally saw her.

The blonde head was bent over an open drawer marked 'confidential,' long fingers flicking through files. Alya's pulse boiled.

"Just what in the hell do you think you're doing?"

Chapter Eleven

The question came out of nowhere and Elle shot up so fast that she barely knew what she was doing until the sharp pain cut her journey short.

"Ow, Jesus, ow."

She clamped a hand to her head. Fine, she'd been spying, scoping out the lay of the land, finding out what she could whilst Goldstein's door was closed and she had a little privacy. But it wasn't like she was going through the woman's purse or anything. Sweat soaked through her shirt at the back, the pain in her head made her dizzy.

"Are you alright?"

Footsteps came closer and then Goldstein was there, close enough that Elle could smell the musk of her perfume, a scent that made her legs shake even further.

"Fine, I'm fine," she said. She must have caught the edge of the upper drawer as she stood up. The pain was biting and sharp. "I was just... Just finding my way around, looking for paper, business cards, all that kind of stuff. Seeing where things were. I'm sorry, I—" She was talking too much, protesting too much.

But Goldstein wasn't paying attention. Her face had paled. "Jesus, you're bleeding."

Elle withdrew her hand to see sticky blood on her fingers. "Shit."

"Come on, come here, sit down."

And Goldstein was pulling at her arm, pulling her up, escorting her to the large chair behind her new assistant's desk. "It's not a big deal, it's fine."

"Blood doesn't seem fine to me, Anne."

Anne? "Um, it's Elle."

"Elle, right. Elle." Goldstein's eyes caught hers and Elle saw a glimpse of something there, fear maybe. Well, she did have an assistant bleeding in her office, that was a pretty good reason to be afraid.

"And it's fine, it feels better already. Let me just get a Kleenex or something." She was hurrying now, talking to fill up space, moving for the sake of moving. Having her new boss so close to her was making her nervous for no reason other than that she was there. Which was stupid.

Then hands were reaching down, and touching her, and fingers were on her skin and Elle felt a tingling that went all the way down her body. A rush of lust to her center. A highly inappropriate reaction.

"It doesn't look too deep." Alya's hands were on her face, twisting her chin around to better see the cut in the light. "Hand me that tissue."

Not knowing what else to do, Elle complied. She wanted to either yank herself away from Alya's hands, or to push herself further toward them, she wasn't sure which. The tissue wiped at her skin.

"Alright, you'll live. It's a scratch, nothing more."

"Right," Elle said. A scratch and a brilliant start to her undercover career. Her first look around and not only did she get caught doing it, but she got injured as well. Awesome.

Alya took a step back and Elle remembered who she was supposed to be and what she was supposed to be doing.

"Um, is there something that you needed?" she asked. "Something I could help you with?"

"No," said Goldstein, looking as though she was ready to run back to her office. "Nothing. I just... I just came to welcome you aboard, that's all." She paused. "Elle." She said the name like she was tasting it.

Elle smiled and Alya hesitated before nodding once and then disappearing back to her office.

As soon as the door closed, Elle groaned and slid down in her chair. So much for being the great journalist. She wanted to bang her head against the desk for her own stupidity, but since her head was already throbbing she decided it might not be in her own best interest. So she satisfied herself with another groan.

Whatever this... weirdness was, she needed to get the hell over it. Okay, Goldstein was attractive. But the world was full of attractive women. It wasn't full of high-profile journalism jobs, so she needed to calm the hell down and focus. And she definitely needed to be a whole lot more careful. Getting caught was the one thing that Kim had warned her not to do.

IT WAS CLEAR THAT BUZZ was home by the banging of the door and the stomping in the hallway. Whatever else Buzz may be, she wasn't discrete. Elle rubbed her eyes, smearing mascara, then peered back down at her laptop screen.

"So? How did it go, big shot?"

Buzz kicked off her shoes and came into the living room and Elle spun round and put her feet up on the coffee table to give her room on the sofa.

"It went great," she said, eyes still glued to her computer.

"Awes— what the hell happened to your head?"

Now Elle did force herself to look away from her work. She grimaced. "Long story."

"Try me, I'm here all night." Buzz had a look of concern on her face.

Elle groaned. "Fine, I hit my head on the drawer of a filing cabinet." She left out the part where she was sneaking around because, well, because even though Buzz did know that she was undercover, it hardly painted her in the best light. It sounded sordid and... just not nice.

"Jesus, that story was so long I almost starved to death waiting for the end," said Buzz, pulling out her phone. "What about ordering some Chinese?"

"Sure," said Elle, going back to her computer.

Buzz typed in their regular order. But Elle's concentration was broken. It had been a good first day, she thought to herself. It had. Okay, so she hadn't uncovered any huge secrets, but she was getting the lay of the land, some solid background stuff. She'd made a decent start.

But she was itching for more info. Itching to know what made Goldstein tick. She was smart, successful, beautiful, a stone dropped in Elle's stomach at the thought of Alya being beautiful. She was all those things and yet... And yet she was still the mystery woman. Which meant there had to be a secret, right? There had to be something that she was hiding, some reason why she never did interviews, some explanation for why she didn't want journalists digging around in her life.

Find that secret, uncover that truth, and... She could hardly breathe for a second. A big break, a successful story, a real reputation as a journalist. The thought was mind-blowing. Even more so because, in the dark of night, she had been beginning to think that the doubters were right. That maybe this wasn't the career for her. Maybe she didn't have what it takes.

"Does she have you working already?" Buzz said, putting her phone down.

"Uh, no," began Elle.

But Buzz was already peering over her shoulder, seeing what was written on the screen. "You've started the story?"

"It's what I'm there for," Elle said, knowing that she sounded defensive and not really sure why.

Buzz shrugged. "Okay, okay. Just... it's not like you to be so eager about things, that's all."

Eager wasn't the half of it. She'd sat down as soon as she'd got home, had gotten started, had written opening paragraph after opening paragraph, deleting it each time, not wanting to settle for anything less than perfection.

"Food's on the way," Buzz said, comfortably. She sighed. "Christ, it's been a long day. And I really need to head out to that dive bar on eighth street later, they've got a new punk band in and I need to check them out. You up for it?"

Ordinarily, Elle would say yes. Ordinarily, she'd be the one persuading Buzz to go out and get the drinking started. But tonight she just wasn't in the mood. "Nah, not for me."

Buzz grunted, but didn't try to argue with her, something that she liked about her best friend. There was never any pressure.

"So, the famous Alya Goldstein is officially your boss?"

"Yep," Elle said, typing in a word and then erasing it.

"Are you going to be able to keep your hands to yourself?"

Elle looked up. "Meaning?"

"Meaning that she's attractive, you're attracted to her, and don't deny it because I'm your best friend and I see everything, and she's your boss so you're going to be seeing her every day. Plus, you're not exactly great at saying no to temptation."

"She's my boss."

"I know, I said as much. She also makes you blush when you say her name. And anyway, I know what she looks like and she's exactly your type. No one else would have you busy as a beaver working during what should be drinking time."

Elle sighed and closed her laptop. "It's fine. I'm fine. I'm an adult and know how to control myself, thank you very much."

"Uh-huh."

For a second she had the memory of Alya's hands cupping her face, those fingers mopping blood from her head, the warmth that spread through her as the woman tended to her. Then she dismissed it.

"I'm there for the story. Nothing more. And I might be terrible with temptation, but even I know well enough to stay away from rich bitches with nothing but money on their minds."

"Not again, Jesus, Elle, not everyone with money is a nightmare."

Elle slid her laptop onto the table. "Fine, fine. I'm going to get plates for dinner. You want chopsticks or a fork?"

She didn't want to fight, not with Buzz. More importantly, she didn't want to think about Goldstein anymore. Not right now. Her head felt all foggy all of a sudden and she hoped she didn't have some kind of a concussion.

"Both," Buzz said.

Elle took herself off to the kitchen, determined to ignore the very existence of Alya Goldstein until at least after dinner.

Chapter Twelve

She'd managed to put it out of her mind for most of the day yesterday. Even this morning she'd locked the memory away and concerned herself instead with what kind of coffee to buy and which shoes to wear. But walking into the office she couldn't stop it, couldn't prevent the flash of an image, her hands touching Elle's face.

Elle.

She wasn't about to forget the name again. Not after the kind of dreams she'd had last night. Because away from her logical mind, in the dark of the night, she'd had some very disturbing thoughts about her new assistant indeed. Thoughts that were far from appropriate. She was blushing now just thinking about them, and a squirming settled into her stomach.

"You'll need to stay late tonight," she barked as she marched through the outer office. As if being rude would detract from the fact that she found the blonde attractive.

"Absolutely, not a problem at all."

Elle's face was shining with eagerness and her smile was genuine and Alya found herself feeling crappy that she'd snapped. It wasn't Elle's fault that she was attractive. It wasn't Elle's fault that Alya had hired her when she should have known better. It wasn't Elle's fault that she was so far proving to be a better assistant than any other that Alya had had.

"Good. I'm working on an investment plan and I'll need it printed up and bound into brochure form to present to potential investors. I'll get you the plan as soon as it's done, but I'll need the brochures by the morning."

"Sure thing," Elle said with a bright smile.

She had a dimple in her chin and her eyes were bright blue, a color like the ocean on a hot day, a color that just begged you to dive into them. Alya growled under her breath and cursed her hormones. Seriously, she needed to get a grip. Not trusting herself to say any more, she nodded at Elle and went into her own office.

She had enough to worry about without this. Enough to work out with the thought of trying to buy out Lars Berger, trying to find the money that would mean she'd own him and not just have to work with him.

And work needed to come first.

THE KNOCK WAS SOLID, not tentative at all, not what she'd expect from an employee worried about disturbing her. For some reason that didn't irritate her as much as she would have thought.

"Come."

Elle sidled around the door, hands full. Just for a second, Alya smiled, then she remembered that she was the boss and she was busy.

"Yes?"

"It's almost two," Elle said. "And, um, you haven't left the office, so I asked Julia at reception and she said you normally ordered from Saladalia on the corner, so I figured it couldn't hurt to bring you something to eat."

She took a breath, the sentence too long and she was blabbering like a small child, afraid that maybe she'd done the wrong thing. But Alya was touched. No one that she could remember had ever just brought her lunch on the off chance. Of course, Elle was probably just trying to be a good assistant, but still...

"Uh, thank you."

"Noodle salad, right?" Elle said, walking forward with the container. "Fork or chopsticks? I brought both."

"Fork," Alya said immediately.

Elle grinned. "Me too. Noodles are just way too slippery to eat with chopsticks."

Alya smiled too, unable to help herself. "Did you get lunch for yourself too?"

Elle nodded.

"Then put it all on expenses. Just save the receipt and turn it in to HR before the end of the month, okay?"

"Right," Elle said.

She looked unsure now, like she was thinking of running away and Alya wanted to be kind, to thank her for the lunch, to make up for being a bitch that morning. Kind but not too kind. A thin line to walk. She gulped. "So, um, you're not from the city, are you?"

"That obvious, huh?" Elle leaned back against the window and sun outlined her hair, turning it golden. "Connecticut. But I got here as soon as I could."

"There's nothing wrong with the quiet life," Alya said, thinking that she'd hate living in Connecticut but not wanting to say so.

Elle grinned widely. "Not if you like being quiet, which I don't. No, the city's the place for me. Shopping, living, concerts, I need to be busy, not quiet."

Alya could believe it. Elle's voice was deeper than she might have expected, pleasant to the ear. She wanted her to keep on talking. "What kind of concerts?"

"Oh, anything at all. As long as it's music. I can't stand death metal, other than that though, I really don't mind. Mozart or Taylor Swift or anything in between."

"Her last album was pretty amazing."

"I know, right? Not at all what I was expecting, but still a killer album."

And then Alya stopped herself. She wanted the conversation to continue, but couldn't let it. She had work to do. Elle was her assistant, not her friend. This needed to stop, but she didn't know how to stop it. She didn't want to offend, didn't want to send Elle away. In fact, more than anything, she wanted Elle to just stay, to sit in an armchair in the corner and curl up with a book and just be present.

Jesus, where the hell had that thought come from?

"I'll let you eat," Elle said, moving to the door. "Bon appetit!"

And she was slipping away and Alya was left feeling odd, like she'd made a connection but not made one, like she wanted this to happen again but didn't.

She needed more friends, that was what it was. That was the first casual conversation she could remember having with someone her own age for months. Yes, she really needed to get out more.

Not with her assistant though. Obviously.

Her fingers itched with the memory of touching Elle's face.

HER FEET ACHED WALKING up the block and rain splashed onto her jacket. She'd had the car drop her at the corner, wanting a little fresh air despite the rain. The dinner meeting hadn't gone well. The man she'd met, one who had been very helpful when she was starting MedSend, had refused to invest further. Not the result she'd been hoping for. And now it was almost ten and she was exhausted and really wanted a hot shower and bed.

She was almost at her building door when someone stepped out of the shadows.

Without thought she spun around, grasping at an upper arm, moving her weight back, ready to strike, before she realized that Elle's frightened face was staring back up at her, skin white and eyes wide.

"What the hell? What are you doing here?" she asked, dropping her hands, letting Elle go.

"You forgot your keys, left them in the office door, I thought you might need them," said Elle, teeth chattering.

"You're absolutely soaked through," Alya said. "Come with me."

She didn't think about what she was doing. Something about Elle every now and again made Alya want to look after her. Elle followed her inside, into the elevator. "You needn't have worried. The concierge here keeps a spare set, and besides, there's always someone at home to let me in," Alya said without specifying who. Elle didn't need to know too much of her private business.

"Oh, I didn't realize. I just saw the keys and then figured you might be missing them. I tried to call, but you didn't pick up so I swung by here on my way home, just on the off chance. I was going to leave them at the front desk of your building."

"Thoughtful," Alya said as the elevator opened again. She let out a breath. Being in a confined space with Elle had been oddly stressful. She pulled out her phone and saw the missed call. The restaurant had been loud, she hadn't heard it.

She took her keys from Elle, opened the door, and beckoned her inside with only the slightest hesitation. Letting someone into her private sanctuary wasn't the way she did things. But Elle was shivering with chill now.

"Come in, take your wet coat off. I'll lend you one of mine and call you a town car to take you home," she said briskly.

"The brochures are finished. All on your desk," Elle said as she shed her coat.

Alya didn't have time to reply before a shuffling sound came from around the corner.

"Bubbale, is that you?"

She groaned. So much for keeping her private life private. "Yes, it's me."

Shoshannah peeked around the corner, her eyes widening at the sight of Elle. "Oh, I didn't realize we had company."

"This is Elle, my new assistant," Alya started.

"I was just bringing the keys that Ms. Goldstein forgot," Elle said, looking at Shoshanna curiously.

"I see," said Shoshannah.

"And she's just leaving," added Alya.

"Right, right," said Elle. She took a dry jacket that Alya was already holding out to her. "I'll go."

"Give me a second," said Alya, pulling her phone out again. She tapped for a moment. "Okay, there'll be a car outside in three minutes."

"Perfect," said Elle. "I'll be going then. Thank you for, um, for the jacket. And nice to meet you," she said over her shoulder to Shoshannah. And then she was bustling out of the apartment.

Alya watched her go. It hadn't been as hard as she'd imagined, letting someone into her home. Okay, Elle had only come a few feet inside, but still, it hadn't been too weird. At least not until her grandmother had shown up. Not that she expected her assistant to be inside her home again.

"She's a nice girl," Shoshannah said. "She'd be good for you."

Alya bit her tongue. No way was she getting into explanations with her grandmother at this time of night. "I need to shower and sleep," she said. "It's been a long day."

"Go on then, off with you," said Shoshannah.

She lifted her cheek for a kiss and Alya obliged. And she could feel her grandmother's sharp eyes on her as she walked away.

Chapter Thirteen

Okay, going to her apartment building hadn't been the smartest move maybe. Especially going without a plan. And it was becoming very apparent that Elle needed a plan. Working for Goldstein was fine, but she wasn't getting close to the kind of gossip that she needed for a great article. Right now she could write something fine, but she wanted better than fine.

Which was going to mean getting even closer to Goldstein.

Her stupid heart skipped a beat. Because that was going to be a hardship, getting close to someone who made her legs turn to jelly.

Not that she planned on doing anything about it.

Not at all.

But at least she had something nice to look at, someone to look forward to seeing. Right up until her identity got blown and then, well, then presumably Alya Goldstein was never going to want to see her again. Alya Goldstein was probably going to want to punch her. Which put any kind of relationship well out of the question.

She tapped into the computer, opening all the files she could find, trying to figure out a way to get closer to a woman that very obviously didn't like people close to her.

"Excuse me?"

It was a nasal voice. When Elle looked up it was clear from red-rimmed eyes that the man had been crying. She cleared her face of any emotion. "Yes?"

"I need to speak to Ms. Goldstein, is she in?"

"Do you have an appointment?"

He had to be someone who worked in the office, otherwise reception would have called her. He shook his head. "But I really need to speak with her."

Elle buzzed the intercom. "Someone here to see you, Ms. Goldstein." She put her hand over the microphone. "Name?"

"Brian Delane," said the man.

"Brian Delane," she repeated for the intercom's benefit.

"Send him in," crackled Alya's voice.

Elle nodded him through and watched him go, saw that he didn't quite pull the door shut after himself. She paused. She was curious, a fatal flaw and part of the reason she'd wanted to go into journalism. To satisfy her innate nosiness. But this was none of her business. This almost certainly wasn't going to help her story. But... But.

She rolled her chair closer, heard voices. Rolled her chair closer still, and then could make out words.

"I have no choice but to hand in my resignation," Delane was saying. "I won't let Sarah go through this alone, and I can't possibly give the job the attention it deserves, so I have to quit."

There was a pause and Elle could imagine Alya's eyes narrowing, imagine her deep in thought. "Slow down a second," the voice said. "I can't just let you resign."

Huh. Now that shouldn't be unexpected. Just as Elle had thought. Business came before people. Money was more important than feelings, more important than whatever was going on with Brian and what she assumed was his sick wife. The wealthy were all the same. Alya was surely going to make him work out his notice, make him train a replacement, take him away from his wife just when she needed him.

"But—"

"But nothing," Goldstein's voice cut back in. "There's no way that you'll be able to survive without decent health insurance, and I'm guessing you've got bills to pay and a mortgage or at least rent.

Resigning your position here might give you time to take care of your wife, but it's going to leave you in the hole financially."

"But—" Delane tried again.

"Hear me out."

Elle craned in further, anxious now to hear what Alya was going to say. She'd been so sure that Alya was going to be angry that now she was confused.

"What I propose is that you take a sabbatical. You'll be on full pay. You won't be required to come into work. You'll entrust the running of your department to whomever you consider appropriate, I'm assuming you have someone in mind?" She didn't wait for an answer, so Elle assumed Delane had nodded. "You might be required to accept phone calls from time to time in order to clear up any issues. Other than that, your time will be yours. We'll revisit the situation in three months. Would that work?"

"Uh, yes, but—"

"No buts, Brian. You're important to the company and important to me. There's more to life than work, and I get that. You do what needs to be done. And please, if there's anything further I can do, don't hesitate to ask."

"Thank you, thank you. I don't really know what to say."

"You don't need to say anything, now get started. You've got the rest of the day to sort your department out and then I don't want to see you again for three months."

Elle hurriedly scooted her chair back to her desk. She was puzzled, unsettled that Alya had turned out differently from her expectations.

THE JOB WASN'T DIFFICULT. She had basic computer skills, she was a quick learner, she thought she was doing pretty well. Which gave her all the more time to plot and plan. This was supposed to be the story that was going to make her career. If she was going to do this, going to lie and cheat and ignore the fact that Alya Goldstein contrary to any expectation at all made her want to do terribly dirty things on the reception desk, then she needed a fantastic story.

A brilliant story.

She needed to uncover whatever dark, dark secrets Goldstein was keeping.

Elle sighed. She'd thought that getting an in, getting the job, would be the hardest part of all of this. But she was just getting more and more confused.

"I need the Juntiq file."

She hadn't heard Alya come in, and she jumped to her feet. "The Juntiq file?"

"Yes," Alya said. "It's over here, isn't it?"

She walked behind Elle's desk. She was wearing a skirt suit today, the pencil skirt skimming down over her long legs, the jacket cut to hover over her hips. As she drew closer Elle could smell her perfume. Musky and rich. A smell that made her mouth dry up and other areas become far less dry.

"Um, I think it's here, actually," she said, moving toward the filing cabinet on her left.

During her reconnaissance of the office she'd more than familiarized herself with where everything was. She reached out for the drawer just as Alya was trying to walk past her. The weighted drawer slid out at the smallest touch of her hand, rattling as Alya stepped back to avoid it.

And then there they both were. Face to face.

There was a tiny scar on Alya's right temple, chickenpox, Elle thought. Her dark hair was swept back as usual, but up close Elle could see a tendril escaping, starting to shift downward. Alya moved slightly and Elle felt the brush of her hip. And those eyes, green and cat-like, were staring into her own and Elle felt like she was falling into them and her lips parted and so did Alya's and just for a tiny moment, a microsecond, she felt herself being pulled towards the other woman.

She couldn't say which of them pulled back first. She did know that a blush had started to blossom on Alya's cheeks, the fine pink visible even on her olive skin. She also knew that she couldn't trust herself to speak or move or do anything else as Alya plucked the file she needed from the drawer and then turned away without another word.

She waited until Alya was in her office before she struggled to her chair, collapsing onto it.

She was no idiot. There was something there. Some connection, some spark, some something. Goldstein had been just as involved in the moment as she was. Something had almost happened. A kiss had almost happened.

And thank all the gods that it hadn't.

She was coming to her senses now.

A kiss? Seriously? Which would have led to what exactly?

If she closed her eyes she could imagine things, imagine Alya, Alya and herself. Could think of how things could be. But the truth of the matter was that whatever her body might be craving, getting involved with Alya personally like that was a bad plan. A very bad plan.

She clicked her computer awake again. She needed to do better. If she was going to be a journalist then she needed to be one. She opened up Alya's agenda.

Alya.

She was slipping more and more often into using her first name.

Ms. Goldstein. She opened Ms. Goldstein's agenda.

Scrolling through the dates and appointments she could see nothing helpful. Onto the next day, then the next, and then there was something that made her stop.

Two hours blocked off on Tuesday evening.

She flicked through to the next Tuesday, same thing.

She opened up the appointment and read the details, eyebrows climbing higher and higher as she did so.

Then she clicked out of the agenda and picked up her phone to text Buzz.

what do you know about roller derby?

The answer came straight back.

prob about the same as you know about male anatomy.

She laughed, dismissed the text and opened up the internet. There couldn't be many roller derbys in the city. And she was going to find Alya's. And then, well, she was a quick learner, right?

Chapter Fourteen

Dammit.

Alya had never been so close to a kiss before in her life. That wasn't the kind of person she was. When she wanted something, she took it. But this, this was different.

And wrong.

She leaned back against the mirror of the elevator.

Life was about more than work. That's what she'd said to Brian Delane, and perhaps it was about time that she listened to herself.

Poor Brian. She'd met Sarah, his wife, at the odd work function. They were devoted to each other. And now, well, she couldn't blame Brian for wanting to be with his wife. The perfect couple. Perhaps the exception that proved the rule when it came to her belief that there were no happy endings. Because Brian had been serious about quitting his job, about leaving everything he'd worked for, just for his wife.

Alya sighed. Her priorities were skewed, she knew that. Over the last few years, building up MedSend, it had been all too easy to cut everyone else out of her life.

It hadn't been intentional. She'd had friends, friends from university, colleagues she'd met when she'd started working. But with the start up sucking away all of her time she'd missed dinner parties and birthdays and get togethers until things got to the point where she just wasn't invited anymore. Which was fair enough.

Now though, now it was time to get things back on track. This foolishness with Elle was nothing more than desperation. She needed to spend time around other people, needed to get herself out there, start having a life outside of the company. Once that happened, she wouldn't be able to dwell on how attractive or unattractive her assistant was.

She was attractive though, said a voice in the back of her head. For a second she imagined those plump pink lips, the way they'd parted so gently, the way they'd moved toward her. They'd be soft, she knew, soft and searching. A pulse started to throb in her stomach.

Then the elevator door opened.

Yes, she needed to get out more. And she would. She pulled out her keys, about to unlock her front door when the door opened anyway.

"Hello, Ms. Goldstein, nice to see you."

"On your way out, Rachel?"

The woman nodded and smiled and Alya wondered just why her grandmother's carer was always grinning. What was the secret to her happiness? She almost asked.

"Your grandmother's doing just fine," Rachel interrupted her thoughts. "Sugar's been good all day, so no worries there."

"Thanks," Alya said, truly grateful. God knew what she would do without Rachel.

"Oh, and there's someone here to see you," Rachel said, fastening up the last button on her coat. "Just on through in the living room with Shoshannah."

Alya frowned, letting Rachel out before heading in, curious at who could possibly be visiting. It was only when she heard voices that she realized there could be only one person that would drop by like this.

She gritted her teeth and considered just going straight to her office and pretending that she wasn't home at all. But that really wasn't fair to her grandmother. She took a deep breath before opening the door.

"Mother."

"Alya, darling!" Ruth stood up and swooped over to her daughter, brushing cheeks and air-kissing her twice. "It's so lovely to see you."

Alya swapped glances with Shoshannah, who shrugged. She pulled herself out of her mother's embrace. "I thought you were in... Cabo?" It was a guess.

"Paris," her mother corrected, sitting down again.

Shoshannah hadn't provided refreshments, Alya noticed. She lightened a little. Her grandmother was always on her side, she had that going for her at least.

"So, what brings you to this neck of the woods?"

She kept her voice calm, didn't show her irritation. Ruth was here for a reason and she wasn't going to be shy about spitting it out. She knew from long experience that the easiest way to deal with her mother, and the fastest way to get rid of her, was to get right to the point.

Ruth paused, looked down demurely, then held out her hand. Naive and innocent didn't suit her mother, Alya thought, as she stared down at the diamond on the proffered hand. She wanted to groan, but she stopped herself.

"Nice," she said with as much enthusiasm as she could muster. Which wasn't a lot. Though to be honest, it was hard to be elated at what could potentially be her mother's seventh husband. There was no guarantee though, since Ruth got engaged at the drop of a hat and un-engaged just as quickly.

"You're going to love Robbie," Ruth enthused.

I doubt it, Alya thought, but she bit her tongue.

"Robbie's already in Hong Kong," Shoshannah supplied, helpfully.

"I see," Alya said, unsure of where this was going.

"Which is where I'm headed in the morning," said Ruth. "I just wanted to stop by first, while I was in town, just to let you know about the upcoming nuptials and, of course, to give you save the date cards."

Alya looked over at the mantel and saw a thick white envelope. This still didn't make quite enough sense though. Her mother could have called.

"Oh, before I rush off though," said Ruth casually. "I would just like to ask a teeny-tiny little favor."

Aha. Here we go, thought Alya. "Yes?"

"It's such a bore, but Robbie's having an awful time getting a visa. I was wondering if you could sponsor him. Through one of your businesses, you know." She smiled up at Alya. "You're so clever, you always were so much cleverer than I. I'm so proud of you, my angel."

It took all she had to hold on to her temper. She breathed in through her nose and out through her mouth. She closed her eyes so that she didn't need to see her stupid mother. All of this, just for a visa sponsorship. As though she would. Her mother's boyfriend wasn't going to work at MedSend, so sponsoring him on a work visa would be illegal.

Not that that would bother Ruth. As far as Ruth was concerned, the world bent to her own will. People accommodated her, always had. It had taken Alya until the age of seven to realize that this was simply because her mother was beautiful.

Beauty opens doors, Ruth had always said.

But Alya was far more used to doors closing behind Ruth as she ran off with whoever was latest in her line of men. Six husbands. Six. Seven if poor Robbie actually made the grade.

Alya's father had been number two. The only one canny enough to get Ruth pregnant. And the only one sensitive enough that he couldn't stand to see Ruth again after their divorce. Ruth and by extension, Alya. Which was unique at least, since the other five ex-husbands buzzed around like flies at a honey pot whenever Ruth was momentarily single.

She had, she'd realized, respect for her father for walking away. Though she'd never really known him and he'd made no effort to contact her when she'd grown. Not that Ruth had been such a stellar parent either.

She opened her eyes now enough to look at her grandmother.

It had been Shoshannah that had raised her. Shoshannah that had dressed her in pretty dresses so that Ruth could show her off and then promptly forget about her. Shoshannah who had comforted her when her mother forgot her birthday or didn't show up at graduation or failed to call.

"No," Alya barked now.

Enough was enough. She wasn't breaking the law for a woman that she saw at most once a year. A woman who couldn't even be bothered to call on her birthday.

"Sorry?" Ruth said.

"No," Alya said again. "I won't sponsor a visa. Now, if you wouldn't mind, I've had a long day and I'm sure you have an early start in the morning."

Ruth painted on a bright smile. "Of course, my darling. Of course. It was lovely to see you again."

Give the woman something, she rarely created a scene. Ruth stood up, gathered her things, bent to kiss Shoshannah's cheek and then hesitated when she got to Alya before giving her a nod.

"I'll show myself out."

Alya waited until she heard the sound of the door closing.

"She is your mother," Shoshannah said gently.

"She's your daughter," pointed out Alya. "And I didn't see you rushing to illegally sponsor visas for her."

Shoshannah sighed and not for the first time Alya wondered just how someone so gentle and kind and giving had ended up with a child like Ruth.

"You'll miss her when she's gone," Shoshannah said, pushing herself slowly out of her chair with great effort. She shuffled over and kissed Alya's cheeks. "Mind you, if I didn't think she'd slap me back I wouldn't mind bending her over my knee for a sound spanking."

Alya laughed. "Good night, Bubbe."

"Good night, Bubbale."

When her grandmother was gone, Alya poured herself a drink. She always needed one after seeing her mother.

Why was her life so complicated?

She still hadn't found an investor willing to give her enough to buy Lars Berger out. She would never learn to deal with her mother. And she was stupidly close to embarrassing herself with her assistant. Needlessly embarrassing herself.

She was back where she'd started before she'd come into the apartment. She needed more of a life. Friends to talk to, people to help her through things, to distract her. She had to balance things out more, maybe then her life would seem better, easier.

Roller derby was really the only place that she met people that were non-work related. So that needed to be her first shot.

Out of all her problems, making friends seemed to be the most approachable. She just had to go about it the right way, to put her mind to it. So, whoever seemed nicest at the next roller derby practice would be her first try. She'd make a connection, invite someone for a drink. Baby steps.

She sipped away at her whiskey, the smoky taste finally starting to distract her from her anger at Ruth.

Chapter Fifteen

"So, what do you think?" Elle did a twirl in front of the door.

"Of the outfit or of your absolutely insane idea?" Buzz asked from the couch.

"Let's go with the outfit, shall we?"

Buzz ran her eyes over the look. Biker shorts with a skirt on top, a flannel shirt tied at the waist, hair up and out of her face. A nod of approval. "I guess it's a good enough outfit to die in."

"I'm not planning on dying."

"Seriously? Have you seen roller derby? It's not exactly the most lady-like of sports."

"And what do you know about it?"

Buzz sniffed. "I've seen it on TV. I'm digging the lesbian flannel thing you've got going on though. Is that some kind of sign? Like, Goldstein's going to recognize that you're into chicks and, um, I don't know, jump you at the roller rink?"

"Not a sign," Elle said, thinking 'maybe a sign.'

It shouldn't be a sign.

And yet she'd made this decision now to get up close and personal, had decided that she was going to try to be more than just an assistant to Alya. And she was telling herself it was just for the story, but... There was a but. The but was that she was feeling excited about going out for the first time in months. Truly excited.

The truth was that she wanted to spend time with Alya. Yes, the woman was good looking. But she was also smart and mysterious and every time Elle patiently wiggled a nugget of information out of her, she found herself wanting to know more.

For the story, of course.

"Elle, you do know what you're doing, right?" Buzz asked.

"Yes, of course." She bit her lip. "Probably."

Buzz sat up. "Mixing business and pleasure is a bad, bad plan. Especially with someone who doesn't even know your real name. Especially, especially with someone whose dearly held privacy you're about to shatter."

"I'm not," Elle said. And this is how she squared herself with all this late at night. "Okay, maybe the story will make her a little less private. But I'm not intending to destroy her or anything. In fact, she'll get a lot more publicity, maybe even get this investment that she's looking so desperately for. My story could be a good thing."

Buzz raised an eyebrow. "So, let's say you find out something juicy. Um, I don't know, maybe she's the secret love child of Bill Gates or something. Are you telling me that you wouldn't print that?"

"I—" Elle stopped herself. She didn't want to lie to Buzz. Her life was full enough of lies as it was.

"Exactly," Buzz said. "You're playing with fire, Elle. I know you too well. You like this woman more than you thought. And at some point you're going to have to decide: the girl or the story. And right now, it looks like either of those could be a terrible decision."

Yeah. Hurt Alya in the process of keeping her job, or lose her job in the process of wooing someone that she didn't even know was really interested in her. Someone that she'd known for days. Someone that could just be a flash in the pan, a hormonal reaction. And yet someone that she cared about hurting, no matter how long they'd known each other. What a choice.

SHE TIED THE LACES of her roller skates, handily purchased from Amazon and delivered just the day before, and wiggled her toes. Not bad. They felt heavy, but not uncomfortable. On the rink, a handful of women were already circling around, spinning and stopping and starting and generally looking like they knew what the hell they were doing. Elle was just thinking about trying to stand up when she saw Alya dumping her bag on a nearby bench.

She'd thought about this. Thought about how creepy it might be for her to just show up, how someone as private as Alya might view her just showing up. And the only solution she could think of was to be on the defensive herself, to throw Alya off her game a little.

"What are you doing here?" She managed to pull off the half pissed-off, half amused tone that she was going for.

Alya looked up and then frowned, a tiny line appearing before her eyes. Elle drank in the sight of her. Tight leggings, tight shirt, every line of her body was on display. Her pulse quickened.

"Me?" Alya said, straightening up. "I train here. You, on the other hand—"

"I'm just doing a trial," Elle said. "I had no idea, I mean, I'm sorry. You don't exactly look like the roller derby type."

Alya raised an eyebrow. "Neither do you just at the moment. That skirt is going to get ripped off you in seconds."

Elle couldn't help but raise an eyebrow back. "Really?" she drawled, the insinuation in her voice very clear.

"Not—" But Alya broke into a laugh. "Not really what I meant. But it's not a great idea to have loose clothing in the rink. People will use it to pull you down, this isn't exactly a girly kind of sport."

"I see," Elle said, looking down at her outfit again. "Any other tips?"

"Try not to hit the ground with your face," Alya said.

She bent back over her bag, pulling out her skates and Elle watched as she bent over to tie them on. The round curve of her backside in the air was enough to make her mouth dry. Jesus Christ. She felt like she was lusting after a cheerleader in high school or something. She tore her eyes away.

"Good luck with your trial then," Alya said.

Elle looked back and Alya was already in skates, already ready. And obviously wasn't terribly comfortable about Elle being there. Crap. This was supposed to be a bonding experience. "Thanks," she said and simultaneously stood up, wobbling on her wheels.

"Uh..." began Alya as Elle attempted to move one foot forward.

A millisecond later she was within inches of doing the splits, her forward leg still moving and unable to get her back leg to keep up with it. The position was just starting to get painful when there was a hand on her arm, lifting just enough that she could drag her feet together again.

"You should probably get some practice in," Alya said, her hand still on Elle's arm. "I mean, being able to at least skate without holding onto the wall is kind of a minimum requirement."

Elle puffed a tendril of hair out of her eyes, more than aware of Alya's hand on her. It was burning through her skin, sending her heart into overload. "I was an ace skater when I was a kid," she said. "I'm sure it'll come back to me."

"Right," Alya said, cool green eyes staring into hers, hand still there, the touch still very much happening.

Elle took a breath, not sure what to do or what to say but wanting more than anything to kiss Alya. But Alya moved, pulling her along now, practically dragging her to the gate onto the rink. She didn't let go until Elle was on the rink surface. Tentatively, Elle rolled forward.

"Okay, not a bad start," Alya said.

Elle looked up to grin and her feet promptly slid out from under her. She crashed to the ground just as the coach blew a whistle.

"Good luck," Alya said, giving her a hand up. The pity and concern in her voice were very palpable.

SHE GROANED QUIETLY to herself as she clutched onto the bench and slowly, painfully lowered herself onto it.

Two hours of practice. Two hours, of which approximately one hour and fifty eight minutes had been spent face first on the floor. She ached in places she didn't know she had. She was pretty sure she'd sprained a finger and her right knee was a solid fifty percent bigger than her left knee. And people did this for fun? She groaned again.

Not only that, but with the hectic, violent nature of the sport coupled with her practically non-existent skating skills, she hadn't seen Alya at all. Well, unless you counted the sight of her fading into the distance as she skated away as seeing her.

All in all one of the worst plans she'd ever had. However she was going to get closer to Alya, this wasn't it.

"Rough out there, huh?"

Elle managed to squeeze out a smile. "Uh-huh."

"Ice will help for the bruises," Alya said. "There's no major damage though, I take it?"

Elle wasn't so sure, but she shook her head anyway. And as Alya bent to untie her skates, she untied her own. She fully intended to throw them into the first trash can that she saw on the way home. Stupid things.

The rink was clearing out now, the rest of the women gone off to their families or to other places. Only the stragglers were left. Alya picked up her bag and heaved it over her shoulder. Elle looked up to smile her goodbye, embarrassed now at the foolishness of her plan. Alya swallowed and she could tell that there was something going on in the woman's mind. Probably about to tell her not to come back, Elle figured. But then Alya spoke.

"Are you coming for a drink?"

The green eyes watched her carefully and Elle's mouth suddenly stopped working. She nodded. And Alya walked off, not waiting to see if she were being followed.

Chapter Sixteen

Alya Goldstein was not known for making dumb decisions. But as she pushed open the door of the bar, she figured that there was a first time for everything.

Reasons not to invite Elle out for a drink: she was an employee; she was attractive; she made her stomach do funny things and apparently made her make dumb decisions.

She knew all of those things, and yet she'd still done it. Why? Because Elle was attractive. Because she'd promised herself that she was going to try harder to have a social life. Because Elle was the only person left at the rink that she actually felt like talking to. Because Elle made her stomach do funny things.

"How about there?" Elle said, pointing toward a table close to the bar.

Alya nodded and changed directions. By the time they were both settled on their chairs she really, truly knew that she was fucking up. This whole situation was impossible and not one she could be in and any way she looked at it, it was going to end in disaster.

"What'll it be?" asked the waiter, appearing immediately.

"Double vodka and tonic." Screw it. If she were making mistakes, she might as well do it right.

"Same," Elle said. She waited until the waiter was gone. "So, I'm guessing that you invited me here to ask me not to come again?"

"Huh?"

The bar had neon lights and they caught in Elle's hair, making it a swirl of red and blue. Her fragile hand was lying on the table and Alya kind of wanted to take it.

"Not to come to roller derby, I mean," Elle clarified. "I mean, it's your thing, I guess you want to get away from work and everything, so, um, don't worry about it. I'll find something else to do."

"More roller derby?" Alya couldn't help but ask with a grin. She'd seen Elle on the floor more than she'd seen her upright.

"Yeah, uh, probably not," Elle said, grinning back. "I don't think it's really my thing."

"What is your thing then?" Drinks appeared.

"Music, like I said. Going out. I read. Watch movies, normal kind of stuff. What about you?"

For a second Alya thought. What did she like to do? Then she shrugged. She might as well be honest, she supposed. "Other than roller derby once a week and work, nothing. I've been too busy building up the company and now, well..." She trailed off.

"Now it feels like the rest of the world has passed you by a little?"

"Yes, kind of," admitted Alya. "I think I just realized that everyone else has moved on, and that my company, as important as it is to me, doesn't really keep me warm at night."

"So you're looking for a partner?" Elle asked.

Alya was about to say something, to defend herself, to change the subject, to do anything, when Elle's phone rang.

"Oops, hold on a second," Elle said, hopping off her stool and drifting off with the call.

She should leave. That would be smart. Wouldn't it? Elle was her assistant. She was an employee. Did that mean they couldn't be friends? Strictly speaking, no, it probably didn't. It might not be the best idea, but friends could work together, particularly considering the fact that Elle was actually good at her job so there was little danger of an uncomfortable firing conversation.

That wasn't the problem, Alya knew. The problem was that the more she saw Elle, the more they talked, the more her feelings grew. She wanted her. It was an unfamiliar feeling. Odd, scary, new. She didn't know how to handle it in the slightest.

Elle was off the phone now, quickly tapping on icons, messaging, Alya guessed. And then she was back in a wave of flowery perfume that made Alya's mouth water.

"Tell me more about you," Alya said, deflecting the conversation. "How did you end up in the city?"

Elle sighed. "It's not the greatest of stories," she said, sipping from her drink.

"You've got family here?"

"And that would be why it's not the greatest of stories."

Alya saw that the direction of things was bothering her, saw that some of the bubbliness had gone and was about to change the subject again when Elle spoke again.

"I grew up in Connecticut, that you already know. My parents are both in the medical field. Surgeons. Rich, white, you know the type."

Alya did indeed know the type. She hadn't had Elle down as a WASP princess though, and she wondered what had changed.

"They cut me off when I was twenty," Elle said, staring down into her glass.

She didn't pry, it wasn't what she did. She held privacy so highly herself that she assumed other people valued it too. But she couldn't help asking. Elle was quieter than she'd ever seen her, smaller somehow and just like when she'd been hurt, Alya felt the need to take care of her, to hold her.

"Why?"

Elle blew out a breath. "I told them that I didn't want to study medicine. They thought that was a terrible idea, that I'd never make money doing anything else. Money is important to them. More important to them than I am, apparently." She hesitated for just a second before following up with something that Alya had been expecting. "And I came out. I don't think that helped either."

There was nothing to say to that. Alya had no coming out story. She'd always kind of known, and when it was mentioned her grandmother, and even her mother, had simply accepted that that was who she was. And so she always felt guilty when she heard a story like Elle's. Guilty enough that she reached down and took the hand.

"I'm sorry."

Elle took a deep breath, took a drink, and then smiled. "It was a long time ago." She tucked a strand of hair behind her ear. "You know, I have to tell you something. I haven't been completely honest with you."

"You haven't?" Alya asked, her attention focussed on their hands. Elle wasn't pulling away. She should move, but she didn't want to.

"I wasn't a great skater as a child," Elle said.

Alya burst into laughter. "No shit?" she said, once she could speak again.

"Yeah, I, uh, thought it might make me look better, safer, if I told you I was. It was dumb."

Alya shrugged. "We all lie. We do it all the time. To others, to ourselves, it's part of being human. We lie even when we don't mean to, we build up these stories about ourselves that we want to be true, and we want them to be true so badly that often we end up believing them."

"What do you lie to yourself about?"

Her drink was already half empty. She felt like she was swimming in dangerous waters and it was terrifying and thrilling all at once. She was so close to being out of her comfort zone, so close to making what would be a terrible mistake, that her heart was beating faster and faster.

"Many things," she said, her eyes still on their hands, her olive skin against the paleness of Elle's. "About who I am, who I want to be."

"How?"

She should stop talking now. She'd made enough mistakes for one day.

"I tell myself I'm happy alone. I tell myself that what I do is more important than who I am."

"And are you happy alone?"

She looked up now, saw that Elle was closer than she'd thought. Blue eyes were watching her. Elle's face looked so smooth that her hands ached to touch it. For a single second Alya understood the world. She understood how her mother could chase this feeling again and again. A warmth overcame her, an exciting, tingling feeling, like the first tendrils of alcohol taking effect, and all she wanted was to feel more of it.

Elle was taking her by the hand, figuratively as well as literally, leading her into talking, feeling, living, and she desperately wanted to follow her. Desperately wanted for this to be more than just holding hands.

Every one night stand she'd ever had came back to taunt her. Every woman she'd slept with just to ease a physical need stood and laughed and pointed. Because she'd thought that would be enough. And only now, as Elle began to smile, did she realize that no one else, no other way, would ever be enough. Not after this.

The waiter glided by the table and Elle's eyes flickered to him for a second and suddenly, Alya could take a breath. Too much. Too frightening. Too dangerous.

She tipped back the rest of her drink, needing an excuse to move her hand from Elle's. And then she almost choked on the alcohol.

"This has been nice," she said, eyes still watering. "But I've got an early start in the morning."

"Ah, right," Elle said.

"So I'd better be going."

She pulled a bill out of her pocket, put it down on the table, grabbed her bag and was fleeing before she could persuade herself not to. And she could feel Elle watching her as she went.

A bad idea, she whispered to herself as the cool night air hit her. A bad idea. But if it was so bad, why had it felt so good to take Elle's hand? So warmly, heart-pumpingly, pulse-racingly good?

Chapter Seventeen

The music was pumping and after finishing her second vodka and tonic, Elle was finally ready to face the fact that she might be in over her head.

"Why here?" Were Buzz's first words as she dropped her purse onto the table.

"Because I was already here," Elle said.

"Right. So, I'm taking it that you didn't break your legs or anything at roller derby?"

"Nope," said Elle. "But you can sleep easy, I won't be going again."

"Not your secret, undiscovered talent then?"

Elle winced as she moved and her bruises made themselves known. "Not even close."

Buzz ordered them both drinks and Elle hadn't wanted to go home, but now she also didn't want to get as drunk as she might normally. "This is my last one," she warned Buzz, as the waiter put another glass in front of her.

"Please yourself," said Buzz. "So, what's up? It's not like you to call from a third rate bar on the wrong side of town, although I'm as delighted as ever to have your company."

Give Buzz her due, she always showed up. No matter what Elle needed, no matter how bad the situation, she was there. Which was why she'd called the second that Alya had walked out

She'd been afraid. There had been such an intense connection there for a few seconds that it had actually frightened her and she'd wanted someone there to comfort her. So she'd called Buzz. But now it all sounded so stupid, even in her head.

"I was here with Alya," she said, knowing that she needed to explain herself.

"It's Alya now, is it? Not Goldstein anymore?"

She ignored the jibe.

Her heart was beating fast again and her mouth tasted of metal but she knew that Buzz was the one person she could rely on. Which meant that she had to be honest. Really honest. And that was never easy. Especially given that Buzz had already warned her about this.

"I think I've fucked up."

Buzz nodded. "I think you might have too."

"What makes you say that?"

"Because you light up a little bit whenever you say her name," said Buzz immediately. "Because you wake up every morning and sing in the shower even though you're going to a job that technically you don't want. Because something's different about you and I've been around you long enough to know that you're starting to lose yourself in her."

Losing herself in Alya. That was exactly what it felt like. She wasn't ready to put any kind of words onto it yet, not real ones, not concrete ones. But she couldn't deny that she might just have crossed a line.

"Why her?" Buzz asked. "You barely know her, Elle."

"I know her," Elle said. "Or I know enough. I've spent days researching her, remember? I know more about her than I know about most people that I date. And okay, I don't know everything, but I'm getting there. I like finding out, I like getting to know her. Why her?"

She couldn't answer the question herself.

"Why her?" Buzz pushed.

"I don't know. I literally don't. Why anyone? Who controls what we feel and who we feel it for?"

"It might be just because you're in close proximity," said Buzz, sipping at her drink. "I mean, that happens, right?"

Elle shook her head. "Nope, it's not that. I'm sure. It's more than that. A lot more than that."

"Why don't you sleep with her? Maybe that will get it out of your system?"

Elle considered this as she took a drink. It wasn't a bad plan, in fact, it had a lot going for it. Not least that she'd be able to touch Alya's skin, to taste her lips to... She shivered. "Maybe," she allowed.

"So, I'm guessing she's not the rich bitch anymore?"

"There are exceptions to every rule." She could recognize her own prejudice. Mostly. She'd heard Alya with Brian Delane, had proof that she put humans before profits. Besides, the woman ran a medical company, obviously she wanted to help people. Hell, as far as she knew, Alya could have grown up on the streets and earned all her money.

"And what about your job in all of this?" asked Buzz. "I mean your real, actual job."

That was where things started to fall down.

An hour ago her phone had rung. It had been Kim.

"Just because you're not in the office doesn't mean you don't need to damn well check in with me," she'd said.

Elle had left the table, watching Alya out of the corner of her eye as Kim reamed her out. She'd then given a brief overview of what she'd had, which even she had to admit wasn't a ton, not when she said it out loud.

"Not good enough, Baker. You're really bending my faith in you here."

"I've already started the piece," she'd said, watching as Alya's long fingers clasped around her glass.

Kim grunted. "Alright, that's better than nothing. Send me what you have."

And she'd hung up. Without truly thinking about it, Elle had quickly sent the manuscript that she had so far to Kim. What she had so far was fine, it was a fluff profile piece, nothing ground-breaking, but more than anyone else had ever got.

Then she'd gone back to the table, back to Alya, not considering the morality of what she was doing.

"My job," she said now to Buzz.

"Yeah, remember? The one you love so much? The one your parents disowned you for wanting to do? The one that you've dreamed of doing pretty much your whole life? That one," said Buzz.

She hadn't thought they'd be that mad. Okay, so she'd put off telling her parents until the last minute that she'd changed her major. And it had been Buzz who'd told her that she really needed to stop living the lie, that she had to tell them the truth. So she'd done it. Over the phone. Like a coward.

It was her biggest regret. Perhaps if she'd gone in person things would have ended differently. With time and distance she knew she hadn't handled things properly. She knew that her parents had had an image of her and she'd shattered that image in one phone call and that perhaps she should have given them time to deal with what she'd said.

But they'd cut off her finances, no more trust fund, no more paying for school, and she'd been angry and, well, things had spiraled from there. And now she had the family that she'd chosen, which consisted mostly of Buzz.

"Do you want to keep your job?" Buzz asked.

"Yes!" The answer came quickly even as the doubts started to creep in. Did she want to keep her job? Yes, yes, of course she did. What a question.

"Then how exactly do you plan on balancing a possible affair with Alya Goldstein and the fact that you've been lying to her about who you are and what you're doing?"

"That would be the sixty four thousand dollar question." Elle finished up her drink and gestured to the waiter for another even though she'd said she was done and that she wasn't going to get drunk. This kind of thorny problem needed alcohol.

"I could ask for the story to be withdrawn," she said, as the waiter gave her a new glass.

"Uh-huh, I'm sure Kim-possible will be delighted with that. You fuck around for a couple of weeks out of the office and then come back without a story."

"Right, so... So, I could ask for the story to be printed without my name." Not a bad idea, and it was definitely something that happened sometimes, she could do that.

"And what about when Goldstein finds out you're not actually a personal assistant but you're a journalist? Think she won't connect any dots there? She doesn't sound like a stupid woman."

"I can handle that," Elle said, letting the alcohol think for her. "I'll figure something out. I'll quit as her assistant and then tell her I got a new job after a few months. That could work. And anyway, there might be nothing between us by then. It's not like we're getting married or anything."

"You're basing an entire fake relationship on a lie," Buzz pointed out.

"It was a lie from the start," said Elle, lifting her glass again. "I'm just redressing the balance. Okay, I'll have to lie a little more, but only to get things to a place where I can be truthful."

Buzz shook her head and took a drink. "I'm not gonna tell you what to do and what not to do, Elle. You've got to decide these things yourself. But you know that all of this sounds crazy, right?"

"Yes." But crazy could work, couldn't it?

"Do you even know if she likes you back? Is she even gay?"

Elle stopped, mouth open to speak but no words coming out. Not something she'd considered. There was definitely a spark there. She thought Alya was interested. But could she be mistaken?

"Come on," Buzz said. "If we're doing this, we're doing it right. Let's have a couple of tequilas and see how things look after that."

And Elle gave up any pretense of being a sensible adult and let Buzz order the drinks.

IT WAS AFTER THE SECOND tequila that she sent the text. She wasn't completely out of her mind, she knew what she was doing. But it was the point in the evening when everything sounded like a good idea, no matter how bad an idea it was.

The text was still on her screen when she woke up the next morning.

I like you. Do you like me?

Short, sweet, to the point, and very, very inappropriate. She read it twice as her head throbbed. And then she saw the little green 'message seen' icon in the corner.

Chapter Eighteen

I n the end, there wasn't really anything to do but go on like normal. A drunken message, that was all it was. It wasn't like Alya had the choice of not going to work, one of the down-sides to being the boss. Even if she did have that choice, she couldn't take it, because what would that say about her? That she ran from confrontation?

So she would act like normal, pretend she'd never read it, never received it, she'd ignore everything and hope it went away. Always a solid plan.

Except, of course, her brain kept reminding her of the instant leap in her heart when she'd first opened the message. That sudden warmth, that flush of exuberance. Things she had to ignore for about ten zillion reasons. Elle was an employee. Alya didn't do relationships of any sort. And it hadn't been meant anyway, had it? So there really shouldn't be a problem here.

Just ignore it.

Her ears were sharp and she heard the outer door open and heard heels on the carpet and she desperately tried to keep her eyes on her computer screen but it was so hard. Particularly when Elle marched straight into her office, closed the door behind her, and announced:

"I meant it."

Alya blinked. "Meant what."

There was a sigh. "Listen, I could pretend that I was drunk and stupid, or that I meant to send the message to someone else, or any one of a million pathetic excuses. Honestly, that was really my first plan. But on the way over here, I started to think."

Alya crossed her legs. She wanted to be angry, but she wasn't. If anything, she was amused. Elle hadn't struck her as the tenacious type, yet here she was. You had to respect that level of honesty.

"Why should I pretend? I absolutely meant it, Alya."

"You meant it?"

"Yes, I like you."

Here's where things got hazy. Alya swallowed. "Okay."

"But I meant both parts," Elle continued. She was breathing faster now. Her cheeks were flushed. "I like you, but I also asked if you liked me."

"Okay," Alya said again, wishing she could communicate better, wishing she could say something, anything sensible. But Elle was leaning back against her door and breathing fast and her cheeks were flushed and the picture was breath-taking.

"It's okay if you don't," Elle said. "It's fine if you don't. But I kind of need to know. I mean, I'm all for humiliating myself like this if it gets me what I'm looking for, but otherwise, well, I probably need to, um, look for another job, I guess?"

Elle's chest was heaving up and down and Alya couldn't tear her eyes away from it.

"So?" Elle asked, almost impatient. "Do you like me?"

SHE HONESTLY COULDN'T think of anything else to do. Okay, she should never have sent the message. But she had and... And she couldn't quite bring herself to regret it. It had only been that morning when, head still banging, she'd considered just quitting right now and walking away from the embarrassment and realized that she couldn't. She couldn't handle the thought of not seeing Alya again.

So she'd done the only thing she could think of to do. She'd screwed all of her courage up into a ball and marched into the woman's office and told as much truth as she could.

The other part, the job part, that was lurking in her head somewhere. But she could do this. Somehow, it would work out. Because love stories always worked out, didn't they? She'd get her name off the story, she'd do something. She'd figure it out and, yes, she'd probably need to lie again, but only a little, and lying for a good reason had to be better than just outright lying. Didn't it?

But now her heart was thudding and her pulse was racing icy cold through her veins and she'd never felt so exposed in her life. She'd asked and Alya, well, Alya gave nothing away.

She just looked with those cool green eyes, her hair perfect, her skin perfect, her life perfect. And Elle figured she must look a hot mess and she was dying a little inside with each second that passed.

Some kind of survival instinct must have kicked in, because eventually she moved.

"I guess that answers that," she said as calmly as she could even though her heart felt like someone had punched it. "I'll, uh, clear my desk."

She'd already opened the door when Alya spoke.

"Wait."

She turned slightly, not daring to hope but not able to stop a little spark burning inside her.

"Wait," Alya said again. "I, uh, I guess I like you too."

I GUESS I LIKE YOU too? That was the best she could do? It was hardly high romance. But from the look on Elle's face as she fully turned around it was more than enough. Whatever wobbling doubts Alya had had about telling the truth vanished as Elle smiled.

"You do?"

Alya sighed and nodded. "Yes. Yes, I do. But..." Another sigh. "Elle, please come and sit down. You don't need to protect the doors against marauders."

With a little bounce in her step, Elle came to sit down and Alya wondered if she was actually going to break her heart. Because as nice as the truth was, and as much as she was telling the truth, simply liking Elle just wasn't enough. Yes, she was pretty, smart, attractive, she made her laugh, always a bonus. But then there was the but. She cleared her throat.

"Elle, you took me by surprise. I wasn't... I wasn't looking for anyone and then you just showed up and yes, yes, I do like you. I don't really know how or why and I sort of wish I didn't, to be honest. But I do. Just because I do though, doesn't mean that, well, doesn't mean that there's going to be a happy ending."

"Why not?" It should have sounded petulant and childish, but it didn't. It sounded like an honest question. Elle's fair hair fell over her shoulders and her eyes were wide and blue.

"You're my employee, Elle. It's inappropriate."

"Then I'll quit. Or fire me. Either way. Whatever works for you."

The answer came so quickly that Alya thought that Elle must have been prepared for this argument. She took a breath. It was her best argument, the most logical one. And if that wasn't going to work then... Then she'd have to be even more honest.

"You'd really give up your job just for the possibility of a date?" she asked, her tone light.

"Yes," said Elle quickly.

Crap. Alya balled her hands into fists under the desk. She hated this, hated having to open herself up. But she owed it to Elle. Elle had walked in here with her heart on her sleeve, the least she could do was reciprocate.

"Elle, I... Well, I'm not really good at relationships. I don't believe in them."

"You don't believe in them?" Elle asked, puzzled. "Yet they obviously exist."

Alya bit back a laugh. "Yes, they do. But, well, maybe not for me." She took another deep breath. "I don't believe in happy endings, Elle. I just don't. And I think it would be unfair to have you accept anything less than that. If that's what you're looking for."

There. Heart on sleeve. Let her make of it what she would. There was silence for a moment and Alya's heart hammered in her chest.

"I kind of agree," said Elle eventually.

Whatever she'd been expecting, it wasn't that. "You do?"

Elle shrugged. "How can there be a happy ending? Either you end up broken up or divorced, or one of you ends up dead and the other mourns. Those aren't happy endings. I do believe in happy middles though."

"Happy middles?" She was smiling.

"Yes," Elle said quite seriously. "Happy middles. Because why deny yourself something just because it's going to end badly? If everyone did that, we'd never eat too much cake or drink alcohol or take any kind of risk at all."

"I suppose."

"The only question is, how long is your happy middle?" Elle went on. "For some people it's just a couple of months. For others it's years and years. But I don't think that part really matters. You don't turn down something that makes you feel incredible just because you don't know how long it will last."

Alya swallowed, she was getting caught up in this. "This makes you feel incredible?"

Elle stood. "You tell me."

She walked around the desk and Alya didn't know what was happening. Not that she would have stopped her. Elle walked around the desk and then stopped, one hand firmly on the back of Alya's chair. She turned the chair a little and then bent, her other hand coming up to cup Alya's chin.

And Alya let it all happen. She let those blue eyes come closer, she let those plump lips come closer, she let Elle's breath tickle her cheek, and in the end, she let Elle kiss her.

It was light and soft and far, far too short. When Elle pulled back, Alya was breathless. All she wanted was to pull Elle back toward her, to have her again, to taste her cinnamon sweetness one more time.

"I'm not asking for a happy ending," Elle said softly. "I'm asking for a happy middle. Hell, a happy beginning would be a start. I know this isn't ideal, and I know it might not be what either of us would have asked for. But I definitely, irrefutably have feelings for you, Alya. And I think you have them for me too. And in this crazy, horrible, terrible world I think we should grab hold of any shred of happiness that we can. You're born alone, you die alone, but what you do in the middle is up to you."

And Alya had no words. But she didn't need them.

She reached up and pulled Elle down again, brushing her lips against Elle's and feeling a hot tingling in her stomach until the kiss deepened and finally, inevitably, she surrendered herself to the idea of perhaps letting someone into her life.

Chapter Nineteen

The adrenaline wore off as she collapsed back into her desk chair. She'd done it, actually done it. Put herself on the line and told the truth and hot damn, that kiss was something she desperately needed more of.

A risky decision, she'd admit it, but one that was going to pay off. She was going to make sure that it paid off. Whatever she had to do, she'd do it because Alya Goldstein was a whole new ball game. A whole new scary, heart-pounding, only God knows where this was going to end up but she was firmly along for the ride, kind of ball game.

Alya was different. Even from that first kiss. First two kisses, to be precise. There were feelings in there, stirring up, that she'd suspected before could exist but had never actually felt. This could, she thought, be it. As in the real deal. The big L.

If she could finagle her way into making everything legit and truthful and above board and not have Alya walk away the second she found out who she really was.

She had a temporary plan though. One that she was going to hope worked out because there wasn't a plan B.

The phone rang and she picked it up. Alya hadn't fired her just yet, and she hadn't quit just yet. To be honest, she was far too busy feeling the remnants of that kiss to worry about walking off the job. And now she was reluctant to have to be away from Alya for longer than she needed to.

"Alya Goldstein's office."

"Hey, it's Julia from reception. Just wanted to let you know that the big cheese is on his way up. He should be with you any minute now."

Ah, Lars Berger. Alya's big meeting of the day. Elle felt selfishly grumpy at the man, though they'd never met. He was the reason that she wasn't currently ripping Alya's clothes off, or having her own ripped off. It was the thought of him that had caused Alya to break their kiss, to postpone anything else until later.

Elle just hoped she wasn't going to back out or have regrets.

The elevator doors opened just as she hung up the phone. A large man with a prominent beer belly stepped out.

"Mr. Berger," Elle said politely. "A pleasure to meet you." She stood up. "If you'll just come this way, Ms. Goldstein's ready for you."

His eyes twinkled and Elle felt the hairs at the back of her neck prickle.

"Hold on, hold on there. No need to be in such a hurry. It's not every day that I get to meet a girl as pretty as you."

Elle swallowed down any kind of response to this. She wasn't about to screw this up for Alya. So she smiled politely and threw mental daggers at him.

"And what's your name?"

"Elle," she said through clenched teeth.

"Elle. The trusted personal assistant, I see." His eyes glinted again. "And someone like you would have access to plenty of privileged information, I'm sure."

"Sometimes," she said carefully, more than anything wanting this to stop, wanting him to leave.

He nodded. "I'm a rich man, Elle. I'm sure you've heard of me." He sniffed, then winked at her. "Rich enough that there could be handsome rewards for any information that I received that was of interest to me."

She wasn't clear on exactly what Alya was up to with this man, but she was no idiot. And her patience finally snapped. "Corporate espionage, you mean?"

He raised his eyebrows but said nothing.

She shook her head, hands shaking in anger. "Let me be completely clear with you, Mr. Berger. I know who you are, and I know what you are. And there is no way in hell that I would have anything to do with anything as immoral, as crass, as damaging as what you're suggesting."

He simply smiled pleasantly. "Quite the hell-cat, aren't we? Well, well, there's no need to get worked up about things. It was a mere suggestion is all. It never hurts to ask. Now, let me see, the beautiful Alya is through here, I take it?"

And he was showing himself through the office door, leaving Elle seething behind him.

BERGER WAS STILL IN Alya's office when Elle judged that it was time to take lunch. A lunch break that she desperately needed. As she left the office she started to run, cursing herself for wearing heels.

It was all of eight blocks to the offices of *Edina*, but Elle was panting by the time she got to the foyer. She had a brief elevator ride to collect herself, and then she was being spat out onto the main floor.

For a second the sights and sounds overcame her. Okay, it wasn't the old fashioned clacking of typewriters and smell of newsprint. But there was something there. The quiet clicking of a keyboard, the glossy pictures on the wall, the board of pages, the smell of perfumes and the secretive conversations. This was her world.

She'd had to make it her world. She'd made every place she'd worked her world. Her family even. Because this was all there was. This was coming home. Maybe not the home she'd first thought of, a magazine lacked the urgent excitement of a newspaper, but still, it was what she had. And she'd missed it, oddly.

"Baker, my office!"

She grinned to herself as Kim strode past. She'd even missed Kim, with her botoxed lips and her too tight blouses. She trotted obediently after her. She was going to have to be smart here to get what she wanted, and that was fine. One thing was very, very clear to her though. There was a line that wouldn't be crossed. Alya kissing her had drawn that line. From now on, she would work no more on the story.

There were limits to how much of a journalist she would be.

"What did you think of the manuscript I sent you?"

Kim fell into her chair and grunted. "Not bad. It's fine."

Elle arranged her face to try and look disappointed. "I think it's all we're going to get."

"Seriously? After letting you swan around for two weeks, this is all I'm getting?"

"It's more than any other publication has ever had," Elle pointed out. "And there's only so close an assistant can get. I mean, it's not like I'm falling into bed with her or anything."

"Have you tried that?"

From the look on Kim's face she was only half-joking. Elle ignored the remark, but her heart skipped a beat when she thought about falling into bed with Alya.

Finally, Kim sighed. "Alright, I guess I have to trust your judgment. If that's what we've got, it's what we've got."

Elle shrugged. "I mean, if it's not enough, I get it. We could pull the story altogether. It's not exactly ground-breaking, I get that. I mean there are no deep dark secrets in there or anything."

Only as she said it did she realize. The deep dark secret. The reason Alya was so private. Could it be, could it possibly be, that Alya was gay? Was that what she was trying to hide?

Elle hated herself for this. Hated that she could see the story in it. No one's sexuality should be news, and yet it was, it was a scoop, it was noteworthy and new and people would take a prurient interest in it and...

And she was going to keep her mouth very firmly shut about it.

"No," Kim said now. "I'm not pulling the story. I'll work with what we have."

Too much to hope for that she'd be let off the hook completely. Elle just nodded. She was still shaking at her realization. That had to be it. Alya had to be hiding something. And what better than her sexuality? The world could be a cruel place, Elle knew that. A place where sometimes it was better to hide for a million reasons. And she couldn't judge, wouldn't judge Alya for doing that.

But what a story it would have made.

SHE WAS BACK AT HER desk and Alya's office door was still closed. She'd managed to negotiate an extra day off work from Kim to tie up loose ends. And in reward for getting the big break on the Goldstein story she'd also been able to convince Kim to let her take ten days of her accrued vacation time.

Which should give her a little breathing room. Time to think, to plan, to figure out a way around all of this. A way that would leave her with Alya, with her heart intact, and with her job still firmly in her grip.

And thinking was exactly what she was doing when Alya's office door finally opened.

It took a second for her to gather her courage enough to look into Alya's eyes. After all, maybe she'd had a change of heart, she'd also had time to think.

"Elle," Alya said softly. "I've been thinking."

Oh God. Oh no. She'd changed her mind. Elle could feel a cracking in her chest. She swallowed and tried a smile, feeling it shaking. "You have?" she asked lightly.

"I have," Alya said.

She perched herself on the corner of Elle's desk and Elle could smell her perfume and wanted to kiss her lips. One last kiss. Just for the memory. Please, let me have that, Elle begged in her mind.

"If we're doing this," Alya continued. "Let's do it properly."

The words didn't add up, didn't mesh with her thoughts and it took Elle a second to understand them properly. "Do it properly?" she croaked, finally.

Alya grinned. "Would you like to go on a date with me?"

Chapter Twenty

It was strange, like crossing over into another dimension. But she'd rolled her dice, had made her decisions. Whatever was going on here, she'd committed to finding out. For better or for worse. There was something about Elle that made her want to talk, made her want to open up, made her want more than a lonely life in a lonely apartment.

She rang the doorbell and the intercom crackled into life.

"I'll be right down," Elle's disembodied voice said.

Three minutes later, there she was. Tight jeans encased her shapely legs, black boots were half-untied, a thick cream sweater showed a flannel shirt at the edges, and her smile, her beautiful, heart-breaking smile. Alya gulped and her palms got sweaty.

"Um, hi." It was like being fifteen and on her first date.

"Hi," Elle smiled back.

"The, um, the car's waiting," she said, standing back to show the car at the curb.

"Hold on a second," said Elle. "Isn't this supposed to be a date?"

Alya nodded, numbly. This wasn't her, this wasn't like her at all. Normally she was comfortable in any situation, normally she was confident and communicative and somehow Elle seemed to drain all of that out of her and leave her a quivering wreck.

"Then let's start off right," Elle said.

Elle's fine hands clutched at her upper arms as she stood up on tip toes and then her lips were there and Alya was falling into the sweet taste of her. The kiss simultaneously made her pulse race and calmed her down. Her own hands started to move, settling in the curve of Elle's waist as Elle's tongue darted out and teased her own.

"There," Elle said, drawing back. "That's better, isn't it?"

Alya grinned. "Way better."

They hopped into the car, Elle already chattering and Alya listening as the car drew out into traffic. She'd hadn't done this for a long, long time, she realized. She'd dated in her late teens and early twenties, but after a string of failed crushes had finally come to the conclusion that she wasn't supposed to be happy, that there were no happy endings. Then work had started, then building MedSend, and then, well, here she was, almost forty and acting like a virgin on her first date.

"Wow," Elle said, looking out of the window. "Are you actually driving me out into the warehouse district so that you can murder me?"

Alya laughed. Elle had that effect on her. For someone she'd known for such a short time, Elle had made her laugh more in two weeks than anyone else she could remember. "Not quite," she said. "We're almost there."

The car was slowing down, and Elle was practically hanging out of the window trying to see where they were going. She realized only at the last moment.

"An escape room?" she said, turning back, her eyes wide with excitement.

"Why not?" said Alya. It had been a spur of the moment decision, but it seemed like a good one. And judging by the look on Elle's face she was into it too. "Come on," she said. "We've got a reservation."

She got out of the car, then paused. Slowly, shyly, she held out her hand. There was a shaking of worry, then a solid warm feeling as Elle took her hand with her own and Alya helped her out of the car.

ELLE GROANED IN FRUSTRATION. "I just don't get it. How can we possibly have time to go through all of these to find the right one?" She stared down into a chest full of large keys.

"Hold on," Alya said.

The game was a good one, challenging, and she'd found herself stuck more than once. Taking a step back and a breath to clear her head she saw what had been right in front of their faces.

"You need to be logical," she said. "There's not enough time to go through every key, which means there must be a clue, and the only thing I can see is that." She pointed to a graphic on the lid of the chest. A circle, a rectangle, then the number three.

"Huh?"

She picked up a key and held it against the graphic. "See, it can't be this key," she explained. "This key has a triangular top, not a circle, it has a cylindrical shaft, not a rectangular one, and here, at the end, four prongs on the key itself, not three."

Elle sat back on her heels and stared at her in amazement. "You know, if I didn't already want to kiss you, I would now. Smarty pants."

Alya grinned back and then they both went to work digging through the chest, their hands occasionally touching as they searched.

IT WAS ALYA'S TURN to groan. The passage in front of them forked into two and she knew that only one direction could be correct. She was damned if she knew which though. The only clue was a seemingly random assortment of magnetic letters stuck to one wall. Letters that she was sure were an anagram, but she was damned if she could figure it out.

"What's up?" Elle said, appearing from a quick look around the previous room for any clues.

Alya pointed at the magnetic letters.

Elle's blue eyes flashed for a second, her brow furrowed and her lips moved in silent thought, then she smiled. She took a step toward the wall and with sure, quick fingers, she arranged the letters into words, and the direction was clear.

"Huh, words are really your thing, aren't they?" Alya said.

Elle paused for a millisecond. "Yeah," she said, finally. "I told you, I like to read." And then she held out her hand and Alya took it, allowing herself to be pulled in the right direction.

"I'M PRETTY SURE THAT we escaped in record time," Elle was saying.

She was sitting astride a bench, a dripping taco in her hand, and in Alya's mind no one had ever looked more beautiful. Her cheeks were pink from the cold and her lips were so kissable.

"I'm not sure about record. But we were pretty fast."

"Always a good sign in a date," Elle said. "That we can work together, I mean."

"Ugh, don't mention work," Alya said automatically.

"Right, sorry, forgot that I was just a lowly employee and all."

For a moment Alya was worried that there was bitterness in her tone, but then she could see from the look on Elle's face that she was being teased. "Not at all what I meant. It's just been a tough day, is all."

"Care to share?"

Briefly, Alya considered keeping her mouth shut. But what was the point in that? If she was going to learn to open herself up, then she had to go ahead and do it.

"Got turned down by another investor," she said. "Which means there's a strong chance that I'm not going to be buying Lars Berger out, and instead I'll need to come up with a way of working with him. Or of hiring his app in some way." She hadn't figured out the details yet.

Elle shuddered. "Bleh, the guy's a pig, I'd never work with him."

Alya let that slide. She didn't talk dirty about the competition, even if she secretly agreed with Elle.

It was later, as they were strolling home through the chilly streets, arm in arm, that Elle asked about MedSend.

"Why do what you do?" she asked. "It's a niche idea, I'll give you that. But why MedSend?"

Alya could feel Elle's warmth on her arm and it comforted her, felt right somehow. It felt like they'd known each other for years rather than just weeks. Like this was where she was supposed to be.

"My grandmother," she said. "She pretty much raised me, and she's diabetic. I saw how difficult it was sometimes for her to go to the pharmacy and get what she needed, and she had me to run around for her. I figured out that a lot of sick people don't have a kid to run errands, or have other things they need to do. A medication delivery service was the best way I could think of to help those people."

"To help people." Elle's step slowed. "So you didn't get into this for the profit then?"

Alya laughed. "No, I didn't," she said. "I'll be honest, I don't exactly come from the bad side of town. I already had money. What I needed was meaning to my life. And that's why I started MedSend."

Elle nodded and they carried on walking. Alya couldn't help feeling like she'd been tested somehow, and she wondered if she'd passed.

Her question was answered when Elle suddenly stopped. Alya stopped too, turning in confusion, and then Elle grasped both her hands.

"I've had a wonderful time," Elle said.

Alya felt a weight lift from her chest. "So have I.

Elle leaned in to kiss her and Alya let the kiss take her, let it go deeper and deeper, her stomach starting to warm, the warmth spreading tendrils down her arms and legs. Her pulse raced faster, her breath came more quickly and she knew then if she hadn't known before that she wanted Elle.

It was the real test. She knew that. They both knew it. If this was just lust, just pure physical attraction, then they should go ahead and

get it out of their systems. If it wasn't, if there was something more...
Well, she didn't dare let herself think about that. Didn't dare let herself
hope.

She pulled back, looking into Elle's face. "Would you like to come
home with me?"

It was late, Shoshannah would be in bed, and now that she'd
decided, she wanted this to happen. Wanted it with every fiber of her
being.

But Elle was biting her lip and then she was shaking her head and
Alya's heart was sinking.

"No," she said. "No, not this time."

"Okay," said Alya, feeling like a disappointed child.

Elle smiled a smile that lit up the night and reached out to stroke
Alya's cheek and her pulse quickened again. "Maybe next time."

And Alya smiled again. Elle was worth waiting for.

Chapter Twenty One

Saturday mornings were meant to be spent in bed. Preferably with someone else, of course, but Elle wasn't opposed to the idea of a nice long solo lie in. Although every time she closed her eyes and thought about that kiss her insides trembled and her libido yelled at her for being an idiot.

You could have gone home with her, her libido pointed out. Yes, said her brain, but then there's the whole emotional attachment thing, not to mention the 'not being entirely truthful' thing. And that's what had sealed the deal for her.

Okay, okay, she wasn't always the most moral of people, she could accept that. But something in her had balked at the idea of jumping into bed with Alya when she still didn't have things sorted out. Quite sorted out. Because she was going to get there. Eventually. She hoped.

She groaned and turned over, burying her face in the pillow just as her phone started to ring. She picked it up without even looking to see who it was.

"Baker."

This elicited another groan. "Kim, it's Saturday morning."

"And you're on vacation, I know," said Kim, not sounding in the least like she cared. "But I'm not. In fact, we had a late meeting last night and there have been some developments." She paused. "I could have called you last night, if you'd have preferred?"

Elle didn't answer. She supposed she could count her lucky stars that Kim had let her have her date in peace. "So what's so urgent then?"

"We got the quarterly numbers in."

A third groan. Three groans in five minutes was not the sign of a good start to the day. The quarterly numbers were the readership numbers that came out once every three months. The magazine, most magazines, lived and died by them.

"We're down two places in the East coast rankings," Kim said.

Close to disaster. Elle swallowed.

"So, I've decided that we're moving up the deadline on your Goldstein story. We're running it in the next issue. That means it'll be out on Monday."

Christ. Elle sat up in bed. That explained the late night then. Kim must have had half the staff working on the story to get it done, edited, and designed in such short order. Her stomach was filled with flitting butterflies. This was not how things were supposed to go, not what she'd planned on at all.

"Uh, I mean, um..." She stuttered. She swallowed, took a breath. "The story really isn't done."

"There's more to it?" Kim asked sharply.

Fuck. No. That wasn't what she meant. "No, but, just, well, that was only a first draft that I sent through really and—"

"And don't do yourself a disservice, you can write Baker, I've never doubted you on that score. It's fine. Now that it's edited, it's more than fine. It's really quite good, in fact."

She was trying to think on her feet and it really wasn't working at all. "Um, maybe we should still delay it though. I mean, wouldn't it have more impact if it came out—"

"No, no delays. The decision's been made," Kim said. "And frankly, I'd have thought you'd have been just a wee bit more excited, this being your first big story for us and all."

Elle seriously considered groaning for a fourth time, but managed to hold it in. "Of course, I am," she said, forcing some brightness into her voice. "I'm thrilled, I mean, I'm really looking forward to it. It's just, well—"

"Yes, having your big story break while you're on vacation isn't exactly ideal," Kim said. "I get that. I remember what it was like to walk into the office after breaking something big, and I can see how you'd prefer to be here to deal with the fallout. But it can't be helped. The story has to be run. Unless, well, unless you want to postpone your vacation?"

Elle closed her eyes. No, she couldn't do that. She didn't want to. She couldn't just walk out on Alya, that would be even worse. Especially if the story was about to break. She took a breath. "No, no, I'm sure it'll all be fine. If there are requests for quotes and such, I can always answer them by email."

"Right," Kim said. "Alrighty then. Well, I just wanted to let you know the big news. I suppose I'll let you get back to your weekend then."

She said the word weekend like it was a dirty word, like she never partook in them herself. Elle wondered if Kim actually lived at the office.

"Thanks," she said, weakly, and hung up.

For fuck's sake.

She'd thought she would have more time. More time to figure out the details, more time to plan just how exactly she was going to come out of this situation with her job and her fragile beginning of a relationship intact. She needed more time. Way more time.

There was a knocking at the door.

"Yeah?"

"You alright?" Buzz poked her head around the door. "I heard groans and thought you might need some aspirin or a bucket or something."

"I'm not hungover," said Elle, wishing that she were, anything would be better than the panic she was starting to feel.

"Oh dear," said Buzz. "Come on then." She came inside and settled on the edge of the bed. "Tell Auntie Buzz all about it."

And it all came spilling out. The wonderful date that had made her forget what time it was, the amazing kiss that had made her forget her own name, not going home with Alya, not having a plan fully formed yet, and then Kim deciding to run the story way sooner than she'd ever expected.

"I'm supposed to have more time!" she wailed.

Buzz patted her hand. "Well, dear, you have been playing with fire, so getting burned isn't out of the question."

Elle stuck her tongue out. "Not helpful. What am I supposed to do now?"

"You could tell the truth."

A shiver of coldness went through her. She could imagine the look on Alya's face. She could imagine the cold, hard words. She could imagine never seeing her again, touching her again, like being banished to the Arctic. "No," she said. "No, I know I'm supposed to, but I don't see how it will help. I will tell the truth at some point, but not now, not while things are still so fresh and new."

She would tell the truth. But in her head, this happened in front of a roaring fire when she was at least seventy and Alya was rocking one of their grandchildren to sleep and by then it was a quirky story, entertaining, maybe even funny.

Buzz sighed. "Elle, come on, this has gone far enough. It's gone way too far, actually."

"I know." And she did know. Things were starting to spin out of control. If they'd ever been under control in the first place. "But I like her, Buzz. Like, I really like her."

Another sigh from Buzz. "You sure?"

She thought about the way that Alya made her skin tingle and she thought about the way that it was so easy to imagine Alya cradling one of their grandchildren and both thoughts made her terrified and calm at the same time. She nodded.

"Maybe you should sleep with her," said Buzz. "Just to be sure. I mean, this could all just be hormones talking, you know? Maybe you'll do the deed and then there'll be nothing left. It's been known to happen."

"I guess."

"Well, it'd be kind of helpful if you were just in lust with her."

The problem with that was that Elle was ninety-eight percent sure that she wasn't just in lust with Alya. The idea of sleeping with her was certainly an attractive one. But still, she had to stand by what she had decided instinctively the night before. There were certain lines she couldn't cross, and she couldn't sleep with Alya until she was at least on the road to setting things right.

Unfortunately, any plans she'd had in that direction had been derailed by Kim bumping up the story.

Unless.

Unless she put her own plans on fast forward.

Okay, she'd thought that she'd have more time, but the simple fact was that she didn't. And now she needed to act fast. So, she'd have to act fast, that was all there was to it.

"I'm going to quit."

She felt better just from saying the words.

Buzz's eyebrows shot up. "Wow, I take it all back, even the things that I was secretly thinking but didn't say. If you're willing to quit your job for the woman, then you must be in love with her."

"No," Elle said with a frown. "I'm not quitting my day job. I'm going to quit as Alya's assistant. Alright, it's not the full solution, but it's the start of one. I can't start being honest until I'm not actually working for her anymore, so that's my first step. I'll quit first thing on Monday and then, well, and then things will play out from there."

She felt immensely better for having made the decision. Lighter and freer and happier.

But Buzz was shaking her head. "You're still playing with fire," she said.

And her voice sounded ominous enough that a chill went down Elle's spine.

Chapter Twenty Two

She hadn't known. That was the worst part. Walking to work that morning, passing people on the street, walking into reception, taking the elevator, all those people had known. And she hadn't. Her first instinct was to feel like a fool. An absolute fool.

Her second response was to be violently sick. Fortunately, she didn't make herself look any worse and made it to the bathroom behind her private office.

And when she looked into the mirror after, her skin yellow and pale, her eyes rimmed in red, the bitter taste of vomit still on her tongue, she felt violated.

Violated.

That was the feeling that stuck.

She, who had worked so hard to remain private, who had closed the shutters and locked the doors and tried to stay the hell out of the limelight, she had had all her illusions shattered.

She'd thought that she could do the job, just the job, that everything else would be fine, that she could keep her anonymity, at least somewhat, keep her private life private. And now this.

She put her sweating hands onto the cool rim of the sink. It had been bound to happen, she thought. The bigger MedSend got, the more people were interested in her. But like this? Taken by surprise like this? Somebody, some sneaky, moral-less bastard of a person had followed her around, spied on her, had finagled out her story without her knowledge, without her permission.

"Well, you turned down every interview," she hissed at her reflection. "What the hell did you expect?"

She chugged some mouthwash, swilling it around in her mouth until it burned, and then spitting it down the drain.

"Alya? Alya? Are you okay in there?"

The knocking on the door was timid but Elle's voice was strong. And Alya found that she felt relief, that she felt a little better knowing someone was there. She pushed back her hair and opened the door.

"I'll be fine," she said, coming out of the bathroom.

Elle looked worried, her eyes big and her skin pale and Alya straightened herself, wanting to look better, wanting Elle not to worry. She strode over to her desk, jabbing her finger at the open magazine.

"Have you seen this?"

Elle bit her lip, but nodded.

Alya grunted and sat down. "Bastards. They could at least have asked for permission. And they had the audacity to send me a copy."

"Would you have given it?" Elle asked. "Your permission, I mean?"

Alya looked up and sighed. "No, probably not."

Elle held her tongue on that but she didn't need to say anything. Alya was good enough at judging herself, she didn't need the help. "What about a coffee?"

"On it," Elle said.

For a second, Elle looked like she was about to say something more. But she didn't. She left and a moment later Alya heard the sound of the coffee machine.

She pushed the magazine away from her in disgust. Slimy, sneaky, bastards. She hated journalists. Hated that she had become fodder for them. And all the article did was reinforce her belief that she should trust no one.

Lars Berger, was her first thought. She'd be willing to bet that he'd had something to do with this. God knew why, but she was sure he had his own end in mind.

She'd just have to be more careful. Trust no one.

She picked the magazine up and flung it into the trash. Where it belonged.

ELLE WAS SHAKING SO badly she could barely carry the coffee to Alya's desk. But Alya didn't notice. She simply thanked her and turned her attention back to her computer.

As always, she'd thought that she'd have more time. After all, Alya was hardly the kind of person that would read *Edina*. But obviously, Kim had messengered her a copy. It was protocol when a big piece came out.

As soon as she'd seen the spread open on Alya's desk a darkness had come over her. She'd known that she'd been wrong. So wrong. She should never have got into this, never have taken the job, never have lied.

But what could she do about it now? Telling the whole truth wasn't going to take anyone's hurt away. In fact, it would do more damage than good, surely? She'd been absolutely, completely wrong. The only thing she could do now was act better, be better, get things back on track toward a more honest future.

"Words aren't deeds," her grandmother had often told her.

And as much as the phrase had annoyed her as a teen, she had to admit that there was a point to them.

It was better to be better, rather than just to make apologies. So that was what she was going to do.

She just thanked God that Alya hadn't noticed the name on the article. Kim had refused to publish the piece anonymously. And Elle Smith wasn't all that different from Elle Baker. Close enough to raise suspicions anyway.

ELLE BOUGHT ANOTHER coffee. Alya's fourth of the day. She set it on the edge of the desk and as much as Alya wanted to touch her and kiss her or just stare at her until the realness of her became true, she didn't. Work was work. She'd promised herself that. Explained it over the long series of text messages that they'd exchanged over the weekend.

But Elle was hesitating.

"Yes?"

"Um, I was wondering if I could talk to you about something?"

"If you make it fast," Alya said. Berger was due shortly. Yet another round of negotiations. Negotiations that she still didn't have the cash to back up.

"Right," Elle said. She sat down on the very edge of the chair opposite Alya's desk. "Um, I think that it would be best if I quit."

It took a second for those words to sink in. When they did, Alya felt a stab of irritation. Quit? Really? Seriously, she was thinking about having 'trust no one' tattooed on her forehead. How could Elle even think about it? How could she let her down like this?

"Uh, why?" was the question that came out.

"I'm thinking about taking a different career track," Elle said, and she wasn't looking at Alya. Her cheeks were pink and Alya felt a wave of lust that she swallowed down.

"A different career track?" This combination of irritation and lust was frustrating and her blood was starting to bubble and boil. "Like what, for example?"

Elle's face turned an even deeper shade of pink.

"Like what?" Alya asked again, voice sharper.

"Journalism," squeaked Elle.

Her blood was boiling and the tension was taut and something had to give. And no one was more surprised than Alya when she started to laugh.

She laughed until tears streamed from her eyes, until she couldn't catch her breath. It took a full two minutes before she could wipe her eyes and speak.

"Thank you," she said. "I needed that. A little soon for joking, but seriously, I needed one bright point in my day."

She looked at Elle. The one bright point in her day. The one thing that was going right in her life right now. Elle looked less pink now, her eyes were wide and Alya longed to kiss her. But not in the office.

"Listen, Lars Berger is due any minute. Let me finish up here and then I'll meet you. Let's say... The Birdcage? At seven thirty? I could use a drink after today."

The phone on Elle's desk was already ringing. Reception calling about Berger, Alya was sure. And Elle just nodded and escaped, practically running to answer the phone.

WELL, QUITTING HAD gone well. Elle checked her watch as she grabbed a table. Seven twenty-four. Alya would be here any minute. And now she had to think of a way to convince her that she hadn't been joking. That she really needed to quit.

She ordered a drink, a strong one.

She thought long and hard about the right thing to say. Thought of different ways of dressing it up. Thought of arguments she could make in her own favor. By the time her watch hands swung to eight, she'd finished the drink she'd ordered. She got another.

Annoyance was starting to prickle.

Her thoughts moved on from explaining things to Alya. Instead she started thinking about her parents. Never a subject that brought cheer to her heart.

She didn't get the text until eight forty five. A full hour and fifteen minutes after Alya was supposed to be there.

She wasn't going to make it. Still stuck in a meeting with Berger. Still working. Still putting business ahead of pleasure, money ahead of people, profit ahead of her personal life.

Elle wanted to throw her glass, but she didn't. Instead, she took a deep, slow breath. Calm down, she told herself. Calm down. This is a one off, that's all.

But she was still mad as hell as she threw down some money for her bill and walked out of the bar.

Chapter Twenty Three

Alya rubbed her face with her hands and groaned with exhaustion. The streetlights streamed through the windows of her office, and she sat in a little bubble of light shed by her desk lamp. In the early days she'd often been at the office until late into the night. She was better about that nowadays. Generally.

She took out her phone and checked her texts. A good night kiss from her grandmother. Nothing from Elle.

Shit.

The meeting with Berger had gone on far longer than she'd expected. He'd been in the mood for game playing, and in her wisdom, Alya had decided that she'd let him play. She hadn't wanted to offend him, hadn't wanted to make him angry, to give him any reason at all not to do business with her.

But it hadn't been until she'd finally put her foot down and practically yelled at him that he'd suddenly started talking sense. Like a small child that needed snapping at. Berger had been testing her boundaries, she saw that now. And she didn't care.

The long evening had been worth it. She'd negotiated a fair price. Slightly in her favor even. And she was proud of herself. All she needed now was the investment to pay that price, and she'd own Berger's drugstore app lock, stock, and barrel. Exactly what she needed. She'd even doodled around with some new logos, ideas that she really liked.

The investment would be a problem for another day, she decided. She couldn't do everything at once, as much as she'd like to.

Her eye caught the trash can. The corner of the stupid, glossy magazine was poking out. She'd thrown it away in a fit of pique, and now she fished it back out again, smoothed the cover. Know your enemy, wasn't that what they said? She sighed, flicked through the pages with her thumbnail. She'd read the article. Find out what was written. Maybe that would give her some idea of who had been spying on her, who had leaked information. Of who she shouldn't be trusting.

Her phone buzzed and she picked it up quickly, heart thudding. But it still wasn't Elle. Just a text from her phone operator. She sucked air in through her teeth.

The truth was that she wanted to see Elle. Wanted to see her badly. It was an odd feeling, one that she rarely had about another person. Elle had made her laugh. Elle helped her take her mind off things. And Elle was rather obviously currently quite pissed off at her.

She tapped her fingers on the desk for a minute, and then came to a decision. Keying in Elle's number, she let the call ring.

"I'M GLAD YOU CAME." She kept her hand around her beer bottle, treasuring the coolness of it and wanting to leap up and kiss Elle but knowing that things were fragile.

"It's late for a school night," Elle said, trying to be light and failing miserably.

Alya cleared her throat. "I wanted to apologize in person. I'm sorry I stood you up. It's not something that I do regularly, please believe me. And I should have let you know far earlier than I did. I was inconsiderate and I'm truly sorry."

"Really?" Elle asked, leaning in so that Alya could see the blueness of her eyes. "I mean, you really don't stand people up regularly?"

"I don't know enough people to stand them up regularly," Alya said, honestly.

"But given a situation where there's a choice between work and personal, you'd put the personal first?"

Alya frowned. She waved to the bartender for another beer, giving herself time to think. "I won't lie to you. It would depend on the situation," she said finally. "But I do try to avoid making promises I can't keep. I acted on impulse today, asking you to meet me after work. Normally I wouldn't do that, I'd be more careful, knowing that I didn't know how long my meeting would run."

"Okay," Elle said.

"It's important to you that I prioritize," said Alya. "I can see that. And that's a fair desire. One I can try and fulfill. I won't stand you up again, you have my word."

Elle smiled now. "Alright, I didn't realize that this was going to turn into a state of the union discussion. But thank you, that makes me feel better."

Alya took a drink as Elle's beer appeared. "And if we're being honest, then I might as well tell you that the reason I made the mistake of asking you out tonight is because I really, really wanted to see you."

Elle smirked and Alya's mouth watered. "Really, huh?"

"Really."

"That's pretty flattering."

"I've been thinking about you all weekend."

"It's been hard not to, with all the texts flying back and forth," Elle said. Her eyes were darkening and her lips looked smooth and inviting.

"Elle, I know I might not have been the most forthcoming person, I know that I thought this whole thing was a terrible idea at first, but..." Alya took a breath. "But I like you. Really like you."

Elle was turning pink again and Alya thought she could see the pulse in her neck and she wanted to grab her, kiss her, throw her across the table.

"I like you too," Elle said, quietly. "But there's something we need to clear up."

"Make it fast," Alya growled, almost crushing her beer bottle with her hand. There was only so long that she could keep herself from touching Elle.

"This afternoon. What I said. I kind of meant it."

There was a long moment of silence and Alya's mouth opened and words wouldn't come out. Then she shook herself back to life. "You meant it? What part of it?"

Elle closed her eyes, took a deep breath, and then began.

"All of it." She held up her hands. "Just let me finish, okay? You can yell at me after. But first, yes, I should quit. It would be better that way, and you know it. Do you have any idea how hard it is for me to not touch you in the office? Just to stare at you all day? I know you have to be feeling the same. It makes a hell of a lot of sense for me to quit."

"Okay," Alya said. "I guess I could call the agency. Get some new possibilities."

"And I meant the other stuff too," Elle said in a hurry. "I know that journalists aren't your favorite people, but that's the only thing I've ever wanted to do. And really, seeing you working in your dream job, doing what you always wanted, helping people, I just want the same."

Journalists. The scum of the earth as far as she was concerned. But Elle had a right to her dreams, didn't she? It wasn't like she could dictate what everyone in her life did.

She took another drink, carefully placing her bottle down.

"Alright," she said.

"What's alright?"

Elle looked like a little girl, biting her lip, barely able to keep still in her seat. She was nervous and it was very, very endearing.

"All of it. All of it's alright. You talk a lot of sense, Elle. I guess that's part of what I like about you. And it's your life, if you want to go into journalism, then I guess that's your right. I can't tell you what to do and what not to do."

A smile was starting to spread across her face and Alya couldn't control herself any longer. She let go of her beer bottle, reached out, took Elle's hand in her own. The contact made her head spin and her breath hitch and her mouth dry up.

"On one condition," she said.

Elle raised an eyebrow and Alya moaned under her breath. This needed doing and it needed doing now. There was no way in hell she could think straight with all this tension surrounding her. And she'd never been particularly patient.

She knew what she wanted, and she was pretty sure that Elle did too.

"What condition?" Elle asked, her voice deeper than before.

She twined her fingers in with Elle's, feeling the soft warmth of her skin, barely able to breathe as she thought about touching more than just hands, as she thought about Elle's skin pressed against hers.

"That you come home with me. That you come to bed with me."

She could see Elle's breath catch in her throat, could feel the desire spinning off her. "Now?"

Alya smiled. "Whenever you're ready. If not now, then soon. Just tell me, give me some kind of sign or something."

Elle picked up her beer bottle and drained it. She placed it gently back on the table, then slid down off her bar stool. Alya's heart about stopped.

"I'm ready," Elle said. She grinned and Alya's heart raced back into top gear. "Take me home."

Chapter Twenty Four

She was unaccountably nervous. Not because she didn't want to do this, but because every single atom of her wanted to do this so badly. And she was afraid that somehow she was going to screw it up.

Her hands were shaking, her legs were shaking, and Alya was so close to her that she could barely breathe, let alone think about what she was supposed to be doing or not doing.

It was freeing, having quit. She was on the road to truth. She could do this now, could give herself permission to finally have what she'd longed after. Yet here she was, waiting whilst Alya opened the building door, feeling like a virgin on her wedding night.

"Come on in," Alya said.

She held the door wide open and Elle followed her in, feet sinking into deep carpet, nodding to the concierge desk, walking with her head held high all the way to the elevator. They stood side by side, arms just touching, a flood of warmth flowing through Elle's veins and she was sure she was about to pass out at any moment.

The elevator door opened and they both made to walk into it at the same time, and Elle laughed and took a step back and her hand touched Alya's and something inside her broke.

"We've got a problem," Elle said, as they both got into the elevator.

"We do," agreed Alya.

Elle's breath came faster. They were thinking exactly the same thing and she knew it. The elevator door hissed and then slowly, slowly began to close and they stood and waited the eternal length of time it took for the damn thing to actually be closed and then Alya groaned.

"I can't wait any longer."

It came out as a growl and Alya was already reaching for her, and Elle was already turning and then their lips were meeting in a burning, crushing kiss that sucked the breath right out of her. And Alya was backing her up and Elle could feel the coolness of the elevator wall behind her as she parted her legs, letting Alya's thigh slide between hers.

Molten wetness spread through her, her underwear clinging to her, and she couldn't remember the last time she'd ever wanted anyone so much. In fact, she didn't think she'd ever wanted this badly.

Alya was kissing her, her hands sweeping over her body, then grasping for her waist, pulling her in and Elle could smell her musky scent, could taste the lemony taste of her, could feel her tongue searching, could feel her fingers pressing into her skin.

Alya's warmth was pushing against her, her torso sliding against her shirt and in turn her bra, teasing her nipples. Alya's thigh was pushing against her center and Elle gasped. Alya pushed harder, grinding her against the wall as her lips pulled back and then began to nibble at the soft skin of Elle's neck.

"Jesus," Elle moaned.

"Jesus good or Jesus bad?" Alya asked, stopping just long enough for the question.

Her heart was beating so fast it might explode out of her chest and Elle could feel the heat rising inside her, could feel the pulse when she pushed down against Alya's thigh and she moaned again.

"Jesus, I think I might..."

But she couldn't finish the sentence. Alya pushed her thigh up and moved it back and forth and Elle's head went back, her eyes closing as she pushed herself into Alya. Alya's green eyes were watching her and she knew that the woman was turned on, knew that Alya was enjoying this, that she wanted Elle to lose all control right here, right now.

And there was a good chance that she was going to.

Her body ached for touch, for direct contact. But she was going to take what she could get and as Alya pushed into her again she moaned and could feel the beginning of vibrations in her stomach and she wanted this so badly and...

The elevator slid to a stop.

"Come on then," Alya said, her eyes sparkling with evil delight. "I promised to take you home. Not just to take you in an elevator."

Elle's lips felt bruised and her body was taut with excitement as she followed Alya out of the elevator and into the apartment. It was just as cool and minimalist as she remembered. But this time she wasn't staring around in awe. This time she was aching with need and Alya wasn't about to make her wait.

She followed as Alya led her down a long corridor, finally opening a door into a bedroom that, had she given it any thought, would have been exactly what she expected. A bed, white, in the middle of the floor. Concealed doors and closets around the walls. A large window, blinds pulled down but not swiveled shut. A dim light from a lamp above the headboard of the bed.

That was all Elle had time to take in.

Because Alya's hands were already working, she was already being pushed back against the door, her skirt was already being pulled down, then puddling around her feet. She gasped as Alya's long fingers tickled against her thighs, then moaned as they skated over the front of her underwear.

"I can't make you wait," Alya said hoarsely. "I'm barely able to wait myself."

A shiver of anticipation passed through her and then that pulse beat insistently between her legs and she took Alya's hand herself, pushing it down her underwear, forcing those fingers to find the sticky wetness within and only then did she allow herself to close her eyes and breathe out.

One breath, two, and that was all it took as Alya's fingers danced over her and her heart beat harder and then the dam broke and her muscles were clenching and Alya was holding her and she couldn't breathe and couldn't talk and couldn't anything.

SHE SHOULD HAVE DONE better. Should have had more patience, should have made her wait, should have waited herself. But from the second Elle had agreed to come home with her, all Alya had wanted was to take her as greedily as she just had.

It had taken her a while to be persuaded, but once she made up her mind about something she wanted it and Elle was at the top of her list. And now, holding her shaking, tremoring body, she felt a strange sense of contentment. She stroked Elle's blonde hair.

"Let's get you to bed," she whispered.

Elle let herself be led to the bed, but once there, she stopped. Alya turned to her and those blue eyes melted right through her and she could feel her blood running hot and she swallowed. She was going to take Elle to bed, going to hold her, feel the softness of her skin, listen to her breathing as she fell asleep. Her own needs could wait. This hadn't been about her, it had been about Elle, about giving her something, about taking care of her.

But Elle had her own ideas.

"We don't have to—" began Alya.

Elle was unbuttoning Alya's shirt.

"Really, I don't expect—"

Elle was flicking open the hook on her pants and pulling them down.

"Elle, if you don't want—"

Elle was standing back, a half-smile on her face, eyes heavy with lust.

Alya felt vulnerable, clad only in black bra and panties, Elle's eyes examining every facet of her, that half-smile mysterious and tempting so that Alya didn't know what she was thinking.

"Really, Elle—"

"Stop," Elle said, looking directly in her eyes. "I want this just as much as you do. You don't need to look after me or pamper me. But you do need to give up a little control. We're in this together, Alya. This has to be about both of us."

Alya licked her dry lips and Elle put out a hand, trailing one finger over the curve of Alya's waist. A bolt of lightning shot straight to her core. Her legs quivered. Then Elle was pulling off her own shirt, shucking off her underwear, revealing pink tipped breasts that made Alya want to suck them. Then there was the feeling of skin against skin, the incredible softness and warmth as Elle pushed her back against the bed until she fell and Elle was on top of her and... and... she took a breath. Calmed herself a little.

Elle kissed her neck, kissed down her collarbone and Alya's heart was starting to pound and she gave one last attempt, gave Elle one last chance to escape this if it wasn't what she wanted.

"Elle..."

Elle stopped, looked up. "You're not my boss now, Alya."

And there was such hunger in those deep blue eyes that Alya understood. Understood that this was about both of them, that Elle was just as hungry for this as she was, that somehow, unbelievably, the most attractive woman she'd ever meant wanted her. Elle didn't move. Alya took a breath, then she nodded.

She relaxed infinitesimally as Elle began kissing down her body again. And she put up no resistance at all as Elle gently parted her legs. She certainly didn't complain when Elle kissed the inside of her thighs. She only moaned as Elle's tongue found her wetness. And she had no breath left for anything as Elle slowly, delicately, teased her towards giving up all control.

Chapter Twenty Five

Elle stretched, a pleasant ache between her legs, then rolled over to see that the other side of the bed was empty. She sat up just as Alya was coming out of the bathroom, suit already on, hair still wet from the shower.

"Sorry, sweetie, I've got an early meeting."

That should have been a brush off, and from anyone else it might have been, but not Alya. She had a glow about her, a sense of completion that she hadn't had before. Elle felt warmer just at the sight of her. Is this how things could really be? Waking up in the bed of a woman she wanted more than she'd ever wanted anything else?

"I'll get my stuff together," she said, swinging her legs over the side of the bed.

"That'd be great," began Alya. Then she stopped, turned. "No, uh, no. There's no hurry. You take your time, get a shower, grab breakfast if you want. I have to run, not you."

Elle arched an eyebrow. "You sure?"

Alya looked a little hesitant, but she nodded firmly. "Sure."

She could recognize the step for what it was, a sign of trust, a big sign from someone as private as Alya. Letting her stay alone in the apartment. Her muscles relaxed a little. Yes, maybe it really could be like this.

Then Alya was kissing her goodbye and she lost all sense of sensible thought for a good five minutes.

HER HAIR WAS STILL damp, she hadn't been able to find a hairdryer, as she wandered into the kitchen in search of breakfast. She'd been a good girl, she thought. She'd curbed all her journalistic impulses and hadn't poked around anywhere. The only reason she'd opened the medicine cupboard was to look for the non-existent hairdryer.

She was just opening up the fridge when she heard someone come in.

"Oh, hello."

She turned to see an elderly woman with sharp brown eyes. Alya's grandmother. She thanked the gods that she'd got dressed before going to the kitchen. "Um, hello?"

The woman sniffed. "I was rather hoping that you were my grand-daughter. But you're not."

"I'm not," agreed Elle.

"Indeed."

There was a pause. Elle felt that she was being watched, judged even. In the end, she had to break the silence. "Is there something I could help you with?"

The older woman sighed. "I was just coming to tell Alya that Rachel is coming in late today."

"And Rachel is?"

"My carer," said the woman. Her eyes turned a glittery shade darker. "Not that I need one. But Alya does worry, so she insists."

"Ah, right," said Elle, not knowing what else to say.

"Which means I won't have my crossword," continued the woman. "Rachel usually gets it for me."

Elle scratched her nose. She was, she realized, at a loose end. She'd quit her job with Alya, and Kim still thought she was on vacation. The day stretched in front of her unexpectedly empty. "I could, um, go get it for you, if you'd like?"

The woman smiled now. "You could."

There was a sense of expectation there and Elle couldn't quite decide what was expected of her until... "Or we could go together? That way you can show me exactly which paper you want."

The woman was positively beaming. "That would seem to be the best solution, wouldn't it?" she said. "Let me just go and get my coat and shoes."

She left and Elle wondered if she'd done the right thing. Possibly Alya's grandmother wasn't allowed out of the house. But she seemed perfectly mobile. And she didn't seem senile in the slightest.

She had time to find and eat a cereal bar before the woman reappeared. "Ready, ma'am?" she asked politely.

The woman rolled her eyes. "Ma'am, schma'am. Call me Shoshannah if you're going to be around for a while." They headed to the door before she asked. "Are you? Going to be around for a while?"

Elle didn't know how to answer that, so she didn't. She certainly hoped so, but didn't want to jinx things. She busied herself calling the elevator.

It wasn't until they were in the elevator that she realized that perhaps Shoshannah had forgotten her name. Alya had introduced them once, when she'd been dripping wet in from the rain.

"I'm Elle," she said, just in case.

"I remember, Bubbale. I'm not as senile as you might think." She grinned at Elle who grinned right back at her, she was starting to like the old lady. "I'd certainly not forget someone as pretty as you showing up so early in the morning. I remember the name of every woman my grand-daughter brings home."

Elle's heart sank a little, a stone settled in her stomach. Of course Alya had a past. She'd be stupid to think she didn't. Still, it stung to think of her with someone else. And here was she, thinking she was all special for being allowed to stay in the apartment after Alya left for work. The elevator stopped and Shoshannah took her arm.

"My sense of humor is a little dark," Shoshannah said as they walked out to the street. "That's what you get for being as old as I am. I was teasing. Alya doesn't bring a lot of women home."

"She doesn't?" Elle asked, starting to feel lighter again.

"As far as I know, you're the only one," said Shoshannah.

Elle blushed.

"She's special, Alya. I'm sure you've noticed," Shoshannah went on as they slowly walked to the news-stand on the corner. "Private. A little... cut off perhaps. It's shyness, of course, though I'm sure she'd never admit it. Or maybe a defense. She was always such a sensitive child. And a child like that given to such a mother, I couldn't think of a worse match. As much as I love my little Ruthie."

Elle stayed silent. She'd learned more about Alya in the last thirty seconds than she had in weeks of research.

"So you'll need to be gentle with her. She's a good woman." Shoshannah stopped and turned her sharp eyes on Elle. "You're a good woman too," she said. "I have a sense for these things. You've got a few things to work out for yourself, but once you do, well, you're not as bad as you think you are."

"I, uh, thank you, I guess," Elle stuttered, not really wanting to think about what had just been said.

"Now tell me," said Shoshannah as they walked together again. "Have you read any Patricia Cornwell?"

Talk of books took them all the way to the news-stand and back and into the apartment again. Elle had added a handful of titles to her to-read list. She helped Shoshannah take off her coat.

"Have you read any of the Rizzoli and Isles books?" she asked.

"Are they bloody?" Shoshannah asked, slipping off her shoes.

Elle grimaced. "Yeah, a little."

"Excellent," said Shoshannah with a wide smile. "I'll add them to my list."

"I've got the first three at home, I can drop them off if you'd like?"

"Perfect, thank you, Bubbaleh. Now, I'll just go and start my crossword and then Rachel should be here any minute."

"Need any help getting settled?"

Shoshannah shook her head. "No, dear. I'm fine now. I've taken far too much of your time, but I do appreciate it. And frankly, I think it was important for the two of us to get to know each other a little. Alya doesn't have many people that care for her."

Elle had never really thought of Alya as sensitive or delicate. She came across as so tough, so business-like. She was untrusting, sure, but sensitive? She guessed it made sense though. It made sense and it made her feel guilty. Even guiltier than before. Because she had taken advantage, hadn't she?

She knew what she'd done. And she knew that if Alya ever found out then everything would be shattered. But Alya wasn't going to find out. She was determined about that. She'd seen the copy of *Edina* in Alya's trash can, Alya had either read the story and not noticed the name, or hadn't put two and two together, or hadn't read the story at all. And the story would blow over as they all did.

Then this, whatever this was, this warm, comfortable, beautiful thing that had started would be able to grow. Prosper. And Alya would have someone to look after her.

She kissed Shoshannah's soft cheek, gathered her things, and then left the apartment.

It was odd to be out at this time of day during the week. Odd to have nothing to do. She felt lost almost. Lost and alone and now she was starting to think. Thinking was bad. If she thought too much then she'd feel even worse and she didn't want that. Not after the night she'd just had. Not after finally feeling Alya's skin, her heat, her wetness. She trembled a little inside at the memory of it.

It was almost a relief though. Almost a relief not to have to think about work, not to constantly be trawling through ideas for stories. And she missed the magazine less than she might have thought.

She reached the corner, crossed the street, pulled out her phone. Screw it. She was technically on vacation, right?

"Buzz, hey, it's me. Feel like playing hooky?"

Buzz laughed. "Give me ten minutes, girl, and I'll be wherever you want me."

Chapter Twenty Six

She nearly never came home to touch herself up before going out again. Not unless there was some kind of unavoidable gala event she had to go to in full black tie. But tonight she had. The thought of seeing Elle again was making her chest feel tight and she wondered if things were going too fast.

They were going fast, she could admit that. But then, she didn't want to slow down. She'd made the decision to let someone in, and dammit, she was going to let Elle in.

She was standing at the door, wrapping a scarf around her neck when her grandmother appeared.

"You haven't left yet, Bubbaleh?"

"On my way now," Alya said.

Shoshannah sighed. "Always in such a rush. You never have time to talk to me anymore."

A twinge of guilt made Alya stop, though she knew that her grandmother was complaining out of habit more than anything else. "What do you want to know, Bubbeh?"

"Everything," said Shoshannah.

"Well, let's see... Some stupid magazine did a story about me and I'm getting nowhere in figuring out where they got the information from. The deal with Berger is going to be off unless I figure out a way to get a cash injection. But, on the bright side, I've had two unsolicited offers from venture capitalists in the last two days. God knows why."

"Probably because you're actually promoting yourself."

"What?"

Shoshannah shrugged. "I know you hate journalists, Bubbaleh, but really, there's a reason business people get their faces out there. It promotes interest, gets people to know who you are. Anyway, that's not what I was talking about. I was far more interested in that lovely girl. Elle and I had a nice chat this morning."

Alya blew out a breath. Here was a conversation she wasn't sure she was ready for. "You did?"

"Mmm-hmm. She walked me out to the news-stand and back, since Rachel was running so late. She's a nice girl. I like her."

Alya hadn't known that she'd been so worried about her grandmother's opinion. But now she felt safer, lighter, nicer. "You do?"

"I do," agreed Shoshannah. "You be careful with her though."

"Grandma, I'm not a dragon. I'm not about to eat her up. And for that matter, Elle's no damsel in distress."

"I'll reserve judgment on that," said Shoshannah. "She is a girl with her own problems to work out though. She doesn't know who she is yet. And you can't love who she is until she figures it out."

"We've been on two dates," Alya said.

"She's spent the night," said Shoshannah. "Not that I mind. You should take your happiness where you can, Bubbaleh. I'm just telling you to be careful. You don't need to wait to have sex, it's not the nineteen-fifties. But you should wait until you know someone's true self before really committing. That's all I'm saying."

Alya shook her head. "I'm going to be late. And stop worrying about me."

"It evens the balance," said Shoshannah. "With all the worrying you do about me, it's only fair."

THE WAITER SLID PLATES in front of both of them and Elle groaned with approval.

"So, Italian food is your thing then?" Alya said, pleased that she'd made a good choice.

"I could eat it every day for the rest of my life," said Elle, sticking a fork into her pasta. "What about you?"

"Um, sushi probably," Alya said with a grin.

"What are you smiling about?"

"Just that we're playing the dating game, asking twenty questions, thirsty for information, it's sweet."

"It's not exactly like we know each other terribly well," Elle pointed out. "Which is fine, I'm not complaining. I'm enjoying getting to know you so far."

Alya picked up her own fork. "You're not wrong," she said. "I mean, I'm not interfering at all, I swear, but you did rather take me by surprise when you said you wanted to get into journalism."

Elle's nose wrinkled. "That was bad timing."

"No, not that. It's just..." Alya frowned. "I don't know. You don't strike me as the journalist type, that's all."

"And what's the journalist type?"

Alya shrugged. "Nosy. Caring more about the story than the person. Abrasive, usually, in my experience. I don't know. You don't come off as the hard-nosed reporter, that's all." She took a sip of wine. "Are you sure that's what you want to pursue?"

There was a tightening around Elle's mouth. Aha, a sign of anger, Alya supposed. New information, something to remember. Not that she'd intended to make Elle angry.

"For somebody that doesn't mean to interfere, you're sounding a lot like you're interfering," Elle said, with an attempt at lightness that she didn't achieve. "In fact, you're sounding a lot like my parents."

Alya looked down at her plate. "I apologize for that. Truly, I do."

Elle put down her fork, took a deep breath, then picked it up again. "It's fine. Not a problem. We have to get to know each others' trigger points, right?"

"Was that our first fight?" Alya asked, smiling a little now.

"Hmm. I'm not sure it counts without any yelling, though we are out in public, so maybe it does." Elle pretended to consider the question, then nodded. "Alright, our first fight. Done and dusted. Which means we get our first making up session, right?"

Alya laughed. Her skin was tingling at the thought of touching Elle again, of having her beside her, of simply sleeping next to her. "Maybe we shouldn't do the making up part in public though."

"Probably not," agreed Elle. "And maybe not tonight. Let's not move things too fast, eh? I was hoping that maybe tomorrow night, or the next night, you might want to come to my place."

Alya was so unused to being the one that wanted, unused to her partner being the sensible one, that for a moment she didn't know what to say. But Elle was right. They had all the time in the world. They should try to do this properly. "Your place?"

"It's not as fancy as yours," Elle said. "And I've got a room-mate. Buzz. She's like family to me. I'd like you to meet her. And, well, you let me slip into your life. I'd like to show you a little of mine. Make sure we're even here, make sure you know as much about me as I do about you."

And Alya was smiling so hard now that her cheeks were aching. How had Elle known just the right thing to say? This was exactly the kind of relationship she needed, the one she'd always thought herself too spoiled, too demanding to have.

She looked across the table at Elle. Blue eyes sparkling, wavy blonde hair loose around her shoulders, a spot of spaghetti sauce at the corner of her mouth, and wondered just what she'd done to deserve this. It had been a risk, sure. A risk hiring a woman she found attractive, a risk following through on that attraction to an employee. But a risk that had been worth it. More than worth it.

All she'd had to do in the end was open herself up to the possibilities.

"I'd be honored to be your guest," she said. "Do you think we could make it tomorrow night rather than the day after?"

"Got big plans the night after, huh?" teased Elle.

Alya leaned in, knowing she was showing cleavage. She let her voice drop a pitch or two. "Not at all," she growled. "I'm just not sure that I can wait that long for you."

Elle's eyes glittered with wanting and Alya felt a twinge of a pulse in her center. She wasn't even sure if she was going to be able to wait until tomorrow, no matter how sensible Elle's suggestion was.

IT WAS CLOSE TO MIDNIGHT and Alya was sitting up in bed and she couldn't sleep. Partly because she hadn't really intended to be sleeping alone, not that she was against Elle's idea of being apart for the night. And partly because she and Elle had kissed like teenagers in the street, a real old-fashioned make out session that had left her pumped up and breathless and now she couldn't sleep.

She'd had the lights off for a while, but it was obvious that sleep wasn't coming, so she'd flicked them right back on again. And now she was looking for something to capture her attention, something to pass a little time until she could try again.

Her eye caught a glimpse of shiny colored paper. Intrigued, she pulled at the corner of the magazine, extracting it from the pile of financial reports it had been buried in.

Edina.

She wondered who or what Edina had been. She sucked air between her teeth. She was getting angry just looking at the cover. But she'd rescued the magazine for a reason. She should read the article, should find out what was said about her.

And what better time than now?

She scanned the night-stand, but the only other reading material was the financial reports and she couldn't face those at this time of night.

With a sigh, she grabbed an extra pillow, propped herself further up, and flicked the magazine open.

Chapter Twenty Seven

Elle straightened the coffee table, collecting magazines into a pile and tapping them against the tabletop to make them straight. She stepped back, took a look, then splayed the magazines out again. Was it better to look like she'd made a huge effort or to look like she was being casual?

She was just debating this with herself when Buzz walked in with a whistle.

"This place looks better than when we moved in. You must have been at it all day."

"Yeah, and cleaning is such my thing." Her back hurt, her feet hurt, the only reason her hands didn't hurt was because she'd been smart enough to wear gloves. She turned to Buzz. "Does it look okay?"

Buzz grinned. "It looks great, the whole place looks great. So calm down."

"And you?"

"I'm here as instructed to play nice for a maximum of fifteen minutes, after which I am supposed to make myself scarce until such a time as I deem you might already be doing the dirty, then I can come home."

Elle stuck her tongue out, which made Buzz laugh.

"Alright, alright. I'm here for fifteen minutes max, then I've got a gig to go to, and a party after that. Whether I'm home or not depends on whether I get lucky or not."

"You can totally come home," Elle said, secretly hoping that Buzz would at least be discrete.

"I'll do my best to stay out of your hair."

Buzz stood up and Elle immediately reached for the couch cushion she'd been sitting on. She plumped it, set it back on the couch, then gave it a sound karate chop across the top.

"What was that for?" Buzz asked.

Elle shrugged. "Dunno. I saw it on the home and garden channel once. I think maybe it makes the cushions look better?"

Buzz grabbed two glasses from the drinks cabinet in the corner and poured a measure of amber liquid into each of them.

"Here, drink this."

"Because?"

"Because you're karate chopping cushions and it's weird. And because you might be getting just a touch overwhelmed here. Are you okay?"

Elle nodded and took a sip of the whiskey and shuddered.

"Sure you're okay? I know this is a big deal for you."

"Meeting you is as close as Alya will get to meeting my mother, or my sister, I suppose."

Buzz rubbed her nose then put her glass down. Elle forced herself not to put a coaster under it.

"And I'm going to behave, I told you."

"I know, I know, that's not it. I love you, Buzz, and I'm sure she will too."

"Then calm down. If she's as crazy about you as you so obviously are about her then, well, then I guess things will work out."

"Do you really mean that?"

Buzz hesitated then sighed. "What do I know, Elle? This whole thing is kind of screwed up, but you keep telling me you can work it out and what choice do I have but to believe you? I still think you're playing with fire, but then I can see how much Goldstein means to you and... And I'm just afraid you're going to end up getting hurt is all, I suppose."

It was Elle's turn to sigh. She was more and more sure that something was happening with Alya, something big. Something about her felt like coming home, it felt natural and normal and... right. And for the very first time she felt a wavering of doubt. Maybe she should tell Alya the truth. Just get it out there. Just say it.

That way they could move on with a clear slate, could build something with a solid foundation.

If Alya felt as strongly as she did, well then, she'd try to understand, wouldn't she?

On the other hand, maybe she wouldn't. Maybe she'd have to let go of Alya forever and she didn't think she could do that. For once in her life she was looking at a future that she wanted, really wanted, and she couldn't endanger that. Why take a risk like that when everything was already starting to work out? She wasn't writing about Alya anymore, she had no intention of writing about her again, so what good could it do to tell her the truth? She'd only be trying to assuage her own guilt, she'd only be hurting Alya more.

"I'll be fine," she said to Buzz. "It'll all be fine."

The bell rang and Elle's stomach jumped and a spurt of nervous adrenaline ran through her veins.

"Start mixing drinks," Buzz said. "I'll get the door."

Elle's hands were shaking as she took out a pitcher and started to measure alcohol into it. This shouldn't be so important, yet it was. It was Alya's first time walking into her life, the first time she'd let a woman come into her apartment as a real guest like this. And she wanted to make a good impression, almost pathetically wanted it.

There was the sound of a throat clearing.

She turned and saw Buzz standing in the doorway, her face pale, her eyes wide and filled with a kind of horror that Elle had never seen before.

Behind her was the shape of Alya, familiar and beautiful and forcing Elle's heart to race faster and harder as she took in the sight, as her eyes moved from that angular face downward, until she saw that Alya's hands weren't empty.

She knew what it was. But the two familiar things together looked out of place and it took her a moment to realize what was happening. A second before she understood just why Buzz looked so awful.

Then the pieces clicked and she froze, her stomach falling down to the floor, her blood curdling in her veins, her breath stalling in her lungs.

Alya was carrying the copy of *Edina* that had been in her trash can. "I, uh, I'll just... Um, I..."

Buzz couldn't even stutter an excuse as she sidled out of the doorway and slid down the corridor out of sight. Elle knew she hadn't gone far, could feel her presence, but her eyes were fixed on Alya.

"I've spent most of last night and all of today wondering what to do about all this," Alya said, almost conversationally. She stepped into the room and carefully placed the magazine on the corner of the coffee table.

She seemed calm. Calm enough that Elle's blood started to flow again. Maybe this wasn't going to go so badly. Maybe it was better that the truth was coming out.

"Elle Baker. Suits you. Better than Elle Smith, anyway."

Elle could say nothing. She followed Alya with her eyes as the dark haired woman walked around the living room, examining it, looking curious even.

"You're more creative than most, I'll give you that."

Elle swallowed. She had to speak, had to say something but she wasn't sure her voice was going to work.

"I, um, I—"

"Stop!"

Alya whirled around and for the first time she was close enough that Elle could see her eyes and she knew then that Alya wasn't calm at all. Her eyes whirled with a dark, frenetic energy that belied her unruffled exterior.

"You come into my life, you lie, you cheat, you get a job from me, a job you don't evidently need. And then you wiggle your way into my personal life. You become who I want you to be, you pretend to be what I need. All so that you can get through my defenses. All so that you can get your story."

"No, I—"

"There is no defense for this. You slept with me, for God's sake. You met my grandmother. Just how far will you go for a story, huh? Is there anything you wouldn't do? Is there?"

Elle didn't dare answer, didn't dare open her mouth.

"You betrayed me. You lied to me. You stole my privacy away. You took my body like it was owed to you. You are despicable. You are the epitome of everything that's wrong with this social media, celebrity obsessed world. You make me sick."

She smiled, but it wasn't a real smile. It was a kind of rictus grin.

"You came into my life and tainted it. So I'm here to have some small measure of revenge." Elle must have looked startled. "Don't worry, I'm not going to hurt you. But you marched into my life, so I wanted at least a measure of the same. I wanted to print myself onto your life too. I want this apartment, your home, to be a place where you have a memory of me."

Her breath was coming faster, her face was taut and Elle couldn't even move.

"I want you to come home and remember me here. Remember that you once could have had something wonderful. Remember that you once made a woman drop her defenses, made a woman fall in love with you, faked a romance, all so that you could get a lousy story. Every time you walk into this room I want you to remember me standing here, and remember what a horrible, terrible thing you did."

And now she had to talk, had to at least try. "Alya, I—"

"I don't want to hear it, Elle. I don't want to hear you, I don't want to see you. I don't want anything to do with you. Can you possibly understand that? Can you understand that you've broken me, that I was starting to let you in, that I was starting to trust you, and all you've done is shown me that I shouldn't let anyone in, shouldn't trust anyone?"

"Alya, please."

"I knew there were no happy endings, Elle." Alya was pale and shaking and grasping hold of the door frame. "But you promised me a happy middle."

And then she was gone, walking away, the front door slamming behind her and Elle couldn't chase her, couldn't call after her, couldn't even breathe.

Chapter Twenty Eight

One of the reasons that Alya had chosen her office was the view. The city skyline spread across the wide window and most days it calmed her and excited her at the same time. Being high enough to see the sky, that was the real sign of success in the city, and she had a quiet pride about her view.

But today it was just distracting her, though she was trying hard not to let it.

"Interesting," said the woman opposite her, flicking through the brochure that Alya had given her.

She was tall, not unattractive. The kind of woman that had enough money to make her noticeable in a crowd. Charlene Carter. Old money. A rich, syrupy southern accent when she spoke. But there was a sharpness in her eyes that Alya hadn't missed.

Mind you, she'd been sure enough about her judgment of Elle, and look how that turned out.

She felt a spike of pain in her chest and her eyes were drawn back to that view.

"I'm not going to play games with you, Ms. Goldstein, I'm liking what I'm seeing."

Alya tore her eyes away from the window once again and smiled politely. She cared about this, she reminded herself. She cared deeply about it.

"I've a great interest in giving back, and I require all of my investments to have some form of social conscience," Carter was continuing.

Behind her, the office door was cracked open. She could see the corner of her assistant's desk. The desk that had so recently been occupied by Elle.

How could she have done this? She honestly didn't know what hurt more. Elle's betrayal or her own stupidity, letting someone in so easily, being so easily duped, giving up her precious privacy at the drop of a hat for a quick lay. She felt sick at the memory of it, shaky and nauseous.

"Long story short, I'm interested in working with you," continued Carter.

Alya snapped back to her. She needed this. This was far more important than any personal nonsense.

"Of course, my people and your people will need to go over the finances and conditions, et cetera, et cetera, the boring business stuff. But I think you and I could cooperate very successfully." Carter reached into her jacket pocket, pulled out a pen that looked more expensive than anything Alya had ever owned, and scrawled a number on the back of the brochure.

Alya reached across, read the number, tried not to let any emotion show at all in her face. It was a big number. Not huge, but big enough. Large enough that the buy out with Berger could go ahead, large enough that she wouldn't have to consider working with the man directly.

"Pending details, do we have a handshake agreement?" said Carter.

The view from the window flickered and then resolved as Alya stood up to shake Carter's hand. She was smiling, saying the right things, moving and breathing and doing everything that she was supposed to. So just why did it all feel so empty?

"I'm looking forward to working with you," she said, as she ushered Carter to the elevator.

She kept the smile until the elevator doors closed and then it dropped.

If she turned her head enough she could walk back to her office without having to see Elle's desk. No, not Elle's desk. She needed to hire a new damn assistant. She should be angry, but she couldn't get there.

She couldn't get anywhere, truth be told. She'd barely slept for two nights in a row now. She was hurting so bad that it had all stopped hurting. She was numb. Numb and empty and tired and...

She got as close as she could to the window, resting her forehead against the coolness.

How could this have happened?

How could she have been so stupid?

How could someone like Elle even live with themselves?

It was a long, long time before she could drag herself away from the window.

SHE TRIED TO BE AS quiet as possible closing the front door, but it didn't work. Her grandmother was already there, sitting in a chair just off the hallway, quietly doing her crossword and waiting.

"I knew there was something," Shoshannah said, looking up at her. "I've had that feeling all day. A grandmother knows things."

"Bubbe, not now, please, I can't—"

"Can't what? Can't come into the kitchen and have the chicken soup that I've been working on all day? I told you I felt something was wrong. Come, Bubbale, eat."

She didn't want to talk, didn't want to rehash things. She wanted to be alone with her pain and her hurt and her humiliation. But Shoshannah was linking arms with her, was pulling along and she could smell the soup in the kitchen. She had no idea how long it had been since she'd eaten. Her stomach growled.

She let herself be sat at the table, let her grandmother place a bowl in front of her, let the tantalizing smell waft up to her nose. She took a mouthful and it tasted of home and comfort. Every time she'd been hurting, every time she'd been sick, her grandmother had made this soup. And just the scent of it now could calm her soul.

"Now," Shoshannah said, pulling out a chair for herself. "Tell your Bubbe all about it."

And suddenly the words were there and they were spilling out and she couldn't hold back the emotions anymore. She had to let herself feel as painful and horrific as it was, she couldn't bury things forever, she just didn't have the strength.

When she was done and her crying had softened and she could breathe again, her grandmother took her hands.

"It hurts so much because you let yourself feel," Shoshannah said. "It hurts because it was real."

She wanted to deny it with every fiber of her being, but she couldn't bring herself to. She'd had real feelings for Elle. "I thought it was."

"You think she felt nothing for you?" Shoshannah asked.

"Of course not. It was all just a ruse, a trick, to get me to open up. A way of getting the story. That was all. And it's... It's humiliating. Embarrassing that I fell for it so easily."

Shoshannah sighed. "There are some people in this world that are evil," she said. "You don't need me to tell you that. There are people who do unforgivable things. But then, then there are people who make mistakes. Terrible mistakes, certainly, but still mistakes. Learning to tell the difference between these kinds of people is something that some of us never master."

Alya felt a burn of anger in her throat. "A mistake? You think all of this could have possibly been a mistake?"

Shoshannah's kind brown eyes looked into hers. "Do you think Elle is evil? Do you honestly at the bottom of your heart believe that you could have not seen pure evil, not tasted it in the air, not even suspected it?"

Alya closed her eyes.

"I can't do this, Bubbale. I'm sorry. I can't dissect things like this, I can't forgive, I can't forget. I see my own mistakes, and those are the only ones I can influence, the ones I can learn from. Perhaps you're right, perhaps it was all a big mistake, a misunderstanding, though I honestly don't see how. But in the end it doesn't matter."

"What does matter then, little one?"

"What matters is that I was right all along. There are no happy endings. I should have listened to my head, not my heart. I took a risk and I'm paying for it. I knew better, I went against my better judgment."

Shoshannah snatched her hands away. "And just who told you that there are no happy endings in life?" she snapped.

Alya shook her head. "No one had to. I could always see it for myself."

"Alya Goldstein, you—"

"No, grandma. No, please. Not now, not tonight. I can't do this. Please. Just let me have a little time. I know you don't want to see me unhappy, but you have to let me process this, have to let me work through things in my head. I'll talk to you later, I promise. But right now, I just need to hurt for a while. Please."

There was a long minute of nothingness and Alya could feel the tiredness pulling her down. Her body felt heavy and her mind slow.

"Go to bed," Shoshannah said finally, her voice soft and sad and loving. "Go on, Bubbale. I'll bring you some cocoa. And no more talking. Just for tonight."

Alya dragged herself up from the table.

She wished it had all been a mistake. Mistakes could be corrected. And she couldn't see any way that any of this could ever be corrected.

She should cry, she wanted to. But there were no tears, only raw, wrenching sobs that she was afraid to let out.

She couldn't remember ever having felt worse in her life.

Chapter Twenty Nine

Walking into the building felt weird. At some point it had felt good, like she belonged here, like she'd found a place. Now it just felt... weird. Like this was someone else's life now, something she'd left behind. Except, of course, she hadn't.

Elle took a deep breath before she got out of the elevator. She wasn't supposed to be here. She was supposed to be on vacation. But she was sick of her own company. Besides, weren't you supposed to move on? Get back on the horse? All that crap?

As soon as she opened the office door silence fell and she could feel every eye on her and then there was the buzz of chatter and she knew, knew that they were talking about her. She held her head up high, she was the talk of the town, this was great, this was awesome. But no matter how much she told herself that, it didn't seem to do the job.

"Ah, Baker. My office, please."

Kim marched past and Elle stared after her. Please? Kim had actually said please? Jesus, she should have written a killer article before this. If she'd have known it was going to turn Kim into an actual human being she'd have gone to the trouble before.

She hurried into Kim's office.

"Couldn't stay away, huh?" Kim said, sitting down. "Can't blame you, I wouldn't be able to either. Don't remember the last time I was away from here for more than a week. Couldn't be without the place."

And Elle wanted to agree with her, felt like she should agree with her, but she just couldn't. It was only coming back that she realized she'd actually enjoyed being away, enjoyed sitting behind a desk quietly, enjoyed... Enjoyed looking at Alya every morning.

She felt cold.

It's just another break up, she told herself. You've done this before. You know how it works. It's not going to kill you.

"Circulation went up by over a third this week," Kim was saying now. "Which is down to you and your Goldstein story. So well done."

"Uh, thanks."

Kim sniffed. "Well, it's as much as you're getting from me, so don't let your head get too big."

"Right."

"You alright?"

The question took her by surprise. And then irritated her. Okay, so she hadn't been sleeping great. Somehow the darkness of night seemed to plunge her into a deep hole of sadness. She cried, a lot, at home, alone in the dark. But she was always up in the morning. A little artful make-up, a smile painted on. She hadn't thought that anyone would notice.

It was just a break-up, after all.

"Absolutely fine," she said with more strength than she felt.

Kim sniffed again and Elle wondered if she were getting a cold. "I gotta say, you surprised me, Baker."

"I did?"

"Not with the writing, the writing I knew you could handle. You've got a way with words, and that's why I hired you, on the strength of your portfolio. But..." She trailed off uncharacteristically.

"Yes?" prodded Elle, curious now as to where this was going.

"But I honestly didn't think you had it in you," Kim finished. "You're a good writer, sure, but you never seemed to have that journalistic nose, that taste for a story, a hunger for it almost. Your pitching is weak and you just never exhibited the sense for what would make a good feature. And then you go and pull something like this."

Fantastic. So she didn't have a journalist's nose. Well, not unless she could fake her way through another impossible assignment like Alya Goldstein's.

The thought of it made her sick. Not just the thought of Alya and the hurt on her face and the pain in her voice. But the thought of doing it all over again to someone else. The thought of faking it, lying, going undercover. She honestly didn't think she could do it again.

"The upshot of all this is that I'm obviously now expecting great things from you, Baker. You've shown your worth, finally. So get back to work. I can't wait to see what you come up with next."

The smile was so genuine, so real, that it took Elle aback. She didn't even recognize it as a smile for a moment. Then she managed to grimace back before fleeing to her desk.

All she had to do was do all of this all over again.

Wonderful.

She'd finally found the secret, cracked the code, she finally knew just what it took to be the great journalist she'd always wanted to be and...

And she felt shaky and sick all over.

"SO, HOW WAS THE FIRST day back?"

Buzz pushed a drink toward her as she slid into the booth and Elle didn't answer. She took the glass, let the smooth coldness trickle down her throat, let the first tendrils of alcohol warm her insides, and then, when she was done, she groaned.

"Huh, that good?" said Buzz.

"I don't even..."

Buzz took her hand and squeezed it. "Want to talk about it, or not?"

"No. Yes. Maybe." She took another drink. Buzz was her family, she told her everything. She had to spit this out. Just... Just what? She was embarrassed, she realized. Not an excuse. She cleared her throat. "Kim called me into her office today."

"Already? She can't be bitching you out yet!"

"No, quite the contrary. She was congratulating me, said she never thought I had it in me."

"So what's the problem then?"

"Well, now she's expecting me to do it again."

"Ah, performance anxiety?"

"Maybe," she allowed. "Maybe." She took another sip and then groaned again.

"We can go home if you want?" Buzz offered.

"No," said Elle. "No, I got this. I can't be buried in my comforter and wishing I was someone else anymore. I should get out. There's only one way to get over a break-up and that's to get right back out there."

"Not if you're not ready." Buzz squeezed her hand again. "You don't have to pretend here, Elle. Alya meant a lot to you. As much as I was against the whole thing, I do know that you had real feelings there for a minute. And to have that taken away, well, it's rough. More than rough. It can take time to get back on your feet. Especially when, well, when you might not have been entirely in the right."

Elle felt her face flush. "There were lines I didn't cross."

"But there were lines that you did cross. You knew how Alya felt about her privacy, so you can't exactly expect her to be overjoyed that you invaded it and lied to her."

"I did the best I could. I didn't write everything, that article could have been much, much worse, but I held back. I didn't reveal her big secret or anything."

"Her big secret?" asked Buzz, confused.

"I didn't out her, didn't mention her sexuality at all. I kept that firmly to myself. In spite of the fact that it would have made excellent news fodder."

"I—" began Buzz, but then she stopped herself. "Right," was all she said in the end.

"I know that it was hardly an ideal situation. But I did the best I could with what I had to do, and, well, it obviously wasn't good enough. And she never even gave me the chance to explain, to defend myself."

Maybe because she'd frozen up the second that she'd seen the magazine, the second that she'd seen the look on Alya's face.

"Elle..."

"I had a job to do, Buzz. Why can't anyone understand that? I was supposed to choose between a woman and my career? What the hell kind of choice is that? It's idiotic. So I did the grown up thing and I compromised and tried to make everyone happy, and look where it got me. Nowhere. Fucking nowhere."

Buzz bit her lip.

She was getting angry now, angry at the unfairness of it all. And tears were prickling in her eyes again. She didn't want to lose it here, not in public.

"You really, really liked her, didn't you?" Buzz asked quietly.

All Elle could do was nod.

"Oh, Elle."

She sniffed and blinked away tears. No, she wasn't doing this in public. She refused. It was only a break-up. She'd done them before. She could handle this.

But she was feeling empty and lonely, even with Buzz sitting right there across from her. She was feeling sad and dark and sick and hopeless. Feelings that even she knew she couldn't drink away.

Everything was trickling away out of her control. She'd risked it all so that she could have everything, the job of her dreams and the woman of her dreams. And she just had to face it. She'd lost. Lost Alya, and from her feelings about the office today, probably lost her career as well. Unless she could come up with another story.

Her stomach flipped over.

No. It was all gone.

Without the thought of Alya, her life seemed small and dark and so, so lonely.

Chapter Thirty

Life went on. It had to. No matter how bitter and broken and empty she felt inside, life had to continue. She had to work, she had to provide, she had to try and build something that would make her life less empty. Still though, she was feeling more and more disconnected. Like she was watching herself from above, smiling and hand-shaking and playing her part. It was an odd feeling.

Signing the papers with Charlene Carter should have been a celebratory affair, or at least something that gave her genuine happiness. Instead, it was just another step toward a goal that no longer seemed defined.

"It's a pleasure to be working with you," Carter said as she stood and shook Alya's hand.

"I'm looking forward to successful cooperation," Alya said politely.

The investment was in order. The Is were dotted and the Ts crossed and everything had worked out just perfectly. And Carter herself was a nice woman, forthright, intelligent, someone that Alya truly was happy to be working with.

Carter bent to pick up her briefcase and glanced down at Alya's desk as she stood up again. "Oh, you're a reader too, although given the story, I suppose that shouldn't be a surprise."

Alya frowned and then caught sight of a copy of *Edina* on the corner of her desk. Apparently, allowing the magazine to invade her privacy had entitled her to some kind of free subscription, because copies just kept appearing in the mail.

"Oh, er, I wouldn't say I'm a regular reader," she said, still trying to be polite.

Carter grinned. "Well, you have *Edina* to thank for your investment. I honestly hadn't considered working with MedSend until I saw your profile piece. It was good, persuasive without making you look like a saint."

"Really?"

"Mmm. You know, getting your face out there isn't a bad idea. I'm aware of the fact that you rarely grant interviews, but to be honest, nobody wants to do business with a mystery. We all like to know at least a little bit about who we're dealing with."

Alya just about stopped herself snarling. "I, uh, don't think I'll be doing any more interviews with *Edina*," she said.

"Oh? Shame," said Carter.

As soon as Carter was gone, Alya dumped the magazine into the trash, where she should have put it originally. Every damn time it came she got a glimpse of Elle's face in her memory, a whiff of her scent, a memory of her skin. And every single time it hurt just as much as the first time.

She sighed. Shoshannah had told her much the same thing about publicizing herself. And she hated that it looked like her grandmother was right. She was a businesswoman, not an actress, not a reality TV star, what right did other people have to know about her private life?

She kicked the trash can under her desk so she didn't have to see the light reflecting off the glossy magazine cover.

ONCE THE INVESTMENT was in, Alya wasted no time in concluding the deal with Lars Berger. The sooner the paperwork was signed, the better, as far as she was concerned. She didn't hate Berger, she'd done business with men far more chauvinist than him. But she was wary of him. He was powerful, rich, and smart, and if he took it into his head to dislike her then he could have a serious impact on her business.

So she smiled and played nice and got all the signatures she needed. Again, a cause for celebration that still felt empty and almost pointless.

She'd stayed professional though and was escorting him out of her office, business done, when he frowned at the empty assistant desk.

"You know, it's always nice to do business with a woman as attractive as you," he said.

Alya swallowed and let the sexism slide. She just wanted him out now, she had what she wanted.

"But I gotta admit I was looking forward to seeing that little assistant of yours. The blonde one?"

"Really?" What else could she say? There was nothing to say to that.

"Yeah, she was enough to brighten anyone's day," Berger said. "Had to fire her did you?"

"I, uh, I mean, yes, sort of."

Though not technically. Technically, Elle had quit. Technically, Elle had probably never really held the job in the first place since she'd signed a contract under an assumed name. Technically, now that she was thinking about it, she could probably sue Elle for... something.

"Hard to get good help these days, isn't it?" Berger said.

"Mmm."

She hadn't hired anyone new. She told herself it was because she hadn't found the right candidate. But she wasn't exactly trying hard. Which was ridiculous. Keeping Elle's desk open like it was some kind of shrine. A shrine to what, exactly? To someone who'd betrayed her trust and lied to her and broken her?

"I'm guessing you didn't have to fire her for disloyalty," Berger grunted.

And that caught her ear. "How so?"

He grinned at her, like a naughty little boy. "Can't do no harm telling you now that the deal's done, I guess," he said.

"Telling me what?"

He shrugged. "I like to get the skinny on who I do business with. And I'll do what I have to do to get a good deal. That's how you become successful. Couldn't find all that much on you, so I asked the little blonde here how she felt about maybe passing a little information on to me from time to time."

Alya's heart thudded in her chest. Berger was grinning inanely. Her mouth was dry and she hardly dared think about what he was about to say next.

"Turned me down though," he said with a trace of regret in his voice. "Too loyal to you to even think about it." He shook his head as though this was a bad thing.

"Right," Alya said, as though it was what she'd expected.

Then she showed him into the elevator and tried to get her heartbeat to slow the hell down.

SHE KICKED OFF HER shoes as she walked through the door, not even bothering to line them up against the wall. She was tired. All she wanted was a hot shower and bed. But she could hear her grandmother in the kitchen, and she wasn't about to be rude to her.

"Hey, Bubbe."

"Hello, little one."

"Everything okay? Blood sugar, meds, anything else I should know about?"

"Everything's fine. Nothing for you to worry your little head about," Shoshannah said.

The fact that Alya already had enough to worry about wasn't spoken. In fact, her grandmother had been quite silent on the subject of her break-up and the resulting aftermath. Perhaps Shoshannah thought she was adult enough to deal with things herself. Or maybe she'd decided not to interfere. As if.

She could see from her grandmother's face that she was dying to say something. But she really didn't want to get into it. Not now. She couldn't dissect herself anymore, wondering what went wrong, wondering how she'd been so stupid. Her eye caught a box sitting on the kitchen counter.

"What's in the box?" she asked, distracting Shoshannah from any personal questions she might be working on.

"Books."

"Aha." She narrowed her eyes. Shoshannah certainly had an Amazon account, but this was no Amazon box. "Books?" she fished.

Her grandmother blushed a little. "Books. Your, um, well, Elle and I talked about books when she was here, and she promised to lend me a few. They arrived today. By mail," she added, unnecessarily.

Alya couldn't stop herself from rolling her eyes. "Great."

"And what?" Shoshannah said. "She should have instead let an old woman down? You would prefer that? That she disappointed me, that she went back on her word? Would that have been better?"

She sighed, but held on to her temper. Just. "No, Bubbale. No, I guess not."

She walked slowly down the corridor toward her part of the apartment. Tired and beaten and all she wanted to do was forget everything that had happened.

And yet the world seemed determined today to remind her of Elle at every turn.

She waited until she was in the shower to cry. When her tears could mix with the water and she didn't have to hide anything.

Again and again she was being reminded of the mistake that she'd made by trusting someone, by letting someone in. She'd thought that the pain would get better, that over time she'd recover, get some sense of herself back. But it just wasn't happening.

It wasn't until she got out of the shower that she realized it was derby night. She should have been flying around the rink, beating and getting beaten. Her one release. But even that seemed far too much trouble.

She thought about Elle bending down to fix her skate, falling face-first for the fifteenth time, wincing as she felt her bruises. And she knew that she'd never be able to go to roller derby again without seeing her face.

Chapter Thirty One

The rough material of the couch pressed against her cheek and itched, but she didn't move. The TV flickered and an ad came on, and still she didn't move. It was nice, she'd decided, to have nothing to do. Just to lie down. To not think. And the TV definitely helped with that. If she tried hard she could zone out for hours at a time and never have to think about Alya or her job or her parents or anything else at all.

"Rise and shine!"

Elle groaned, but Buzz stomped into the room anyway. "What?"

Buzz picked up Elle's legs and sat down on the couch, putting her legs back in her lap. "There's a new bar opening up-town. VIP guest list. And guess who's on it? You and me, baby."

Another groan. "No, I'm all good."

Buzz sighed. "Seriously? Come on, Elle. You gotta snap out of this. I know that you're hurting, I know that you're confused. But you're not helping things by moping around the house. You need to get out there, get back on the horse or whatever."

"Yes, you're right. I've had my heart broken. I just need to find some other woman to screw." She regretted the bitterness of the words the second they came out of her mouth.

"Okay," Buzz said slowly, like she was trying to hold on to her temper. "Fine. I get it. You're not ready for that. But you should come out anyway. You're not going to come up with any story ideas stuck in front of the TV. So come out and live a little. See what the rest of the world is doing."

Elle took a deep breath, holding on to her own temper this time. "No, thank you," she said. "I'm just fine here."

There was a long silence, then Buzz stood up and left the room and Elle was alone again.

Just the way she was obviously supposed to be.

How did a life fall apart, she wondered. Just how was it that one minute everything could be fine and the next you felt like you were standing on quicksand and being sucked down and smothered? The TV switched back to regular programming and she let herself be distracted from thinking again.

FIFTEEN MINUTES LATER biological necessity meant she had to actually stand up. After the bathroom she swung by the kitchen. She might as well get a bottle of water while she was up. That way she wouldn't have to get up again until the next bathroom break.

"I'd have thought you were gone already," she said, surprised to see Buzz in the kitchen.

Buzz leaned back against the counter. "Reconsider," she said. "Please, Elle. I'm starting to get worried about you. Please come out with me. You might not enjoy it, it might be terrible, but at least you'll be outside the apartment. Ten minutes, fifteen maybe. I'll come straight back home with you when you're ready."

"I'm already ready," pointed out Elle, pulling open the fridge. "I'm already home. Why should I get ready and go out when I know that I'm already where I want to be?"

"Because it's healthy to go out sometimes."

"I go to work."

"You disappear in the morning and slink back early in the afternoons."

"So? I'm going, aren't I?" She stood up from the fridge, water bottle in hand. "Why are you being such a pain in the ass about this? Why can't you just leave me alone? Fine, I get that you're worried. But I'm dealing with things, I'm healing or whatever. Just go out and do your thing, you don't need to interfere here."

"I'm interfering because I'm worried. I've never seen you like this."

Elle's patience snapped. "Then don't damn well look at me!"

"Elle…"

She breathed in through her nose then out. This was Buzz. Buzz who cared, Buzz who was her family. "I've had my heart broken, Buzz. Just let me live through this one."

Buzz shook her head and Elle saw a glint in her eye and suddenly she wasn't so calm anymore. She knew Buzz well enough to know when she was being judged.

"What?" she asked through gritted teeth.

"Nothing," Buzz said.

"What? Just spit it out, whatever the hell it is that you're thinking."

Buzz stared at her for a long minute then shrugged. "Fine. Okay. You didn't have your heart broken."

"What the hell are you talking ab—"

"You didn't have your heart broken because you broke your own damn heart," Buzz spat.

Elle took a step backward, feeling the cool of the refrigerator behind her back, as though she'd been slapped. "Buzz—"

"No," Buzz said, folding her arms. "It's time for a little tough love here, Elle. And you know that I love you, I truly do. But you need to hear some home truths and if I have to be the one to tell them, then so be it."

"What kind of home truths?" she asked cautiously. She should be angry, she was angry, but she was also shocked and far too surprised by Buzz suddenly turning on her to explode.

"You're full of excuses and justifications, Elle. You were just doing your job, you didn't out Alya, you didn't have any choice in the matter. But the truth is that you did have a choice. You had choices all along the way, you just chose to stick with the path that took you where you thought you wanted to go. And now you're sitting around heart-broken and sad because your own choices led to your own unhappiness."

Elle gulped, felt tears stinging in her eyes. But Buzz wasn't done yet.

"You do the same thing that you always do, Elle. You never admit that you're wrong. There's always some kind of extenuating circumstances, when the truth is that sometimes you just make the wrong damn decisions."

She stepped forward now and from the flush in her cheeks Elle could see that she was truly mad. She couldn't think of the last time she'd seen Buzz like this, seen her angry at all, in fact.

"You're stubborn and blind, Elle, two things that are going to get you nowhere in life. You think your life is falling apart? Well, maybe that's because you refuse to listen to anyone else, maybe that's because you make bad decisions and then stick to them like glue."

"Like what?" Elle said, finally finding her voice.

"What about like being a damn journalist?" Buzz said. "Your parents tried to tell you that it wouldn't be a good fit. The three newspapers that fired you tried to tell you it wasn't a good fit. Hell, Kim-possible has done her best to show you you're not a good fit. Yet here you are, still going to work every day, still not coming up with a new plan. Even though deep inside you know that this isn't for you."

"It is, I just—"

"No," Buzz said. "It's not. I know you too well for this bullshit. You're sitting around here moping and knowing that you can't replicate this story. You can't sneak around, you can't lie, you can't compromise yourself to get the next big story because that's just not who you are."

Her legs were shaking. It was like Buzz was plumbing into the dark depths of her head, speaking aloud words that Elle knew were true but that didn't mean she wanted to hear them.

"And this whole business with Alya," continued Buzz. "I don't doubt that you like her. But you put your job ahead of her, you put your job ahead of your own morals and sensibilities. Which, just by the way, is what you're always accusing your parents of doing, rich assholes putting money and career ahead of personal feelings, right?"

She didn't answer. She felt sick.

"Then you just go and do the same. Is it any wonder that you're unhappy?"

Buzz finally paused. Her face seemed to soften. Elle blinked back tears.

"We all make mistakes in life, Elle. It's normal, it's natural. But when you make them, you have to go back and try and fix things. You have to learn from them. You don't just keep going regardless."

"Buzz—"

"I love you, Elle. But you have to change. You have to start finding happiness, instead of assuming it will come if you follow a certain path. If you keep being so stubborn and hard-headed you'll never be happy. You didn't get your heart broken, Elle. You were an asshole. Just admit it."

She felt herself frowning.

"Go ahead," Buzz said softly. "Say it out loud. No excuses, no justifications. Admit it."

Her lips moved, but no sound came out. She swallowed and tried again. "I was an asshole."

Buzz smiled. "See? That's the first step."

But Elle was already thinking, was already taking everything in, trying to digest what Buzz had told her, examining this shiny new truth that she'd been handed. And whichever way she looked at it, there was only one thing that she could see. One face, one smile, one breath-takingly beautiful silhouette.

She'd been wrong. Wrong about so many things. She was stubborn. She saw it all so clearly. Maybe she'd just needed someone like Buzz to put it all into words for her. And she wasn't going to make excuses for it, she wasn't going to justify her wrong-ness. She was going to accept it.

There was one burning thing that she needed to know though. And Buzz was still half-smiling at her and for once she looked to someone else for an answer.

"How do I fix this?" she asked. "How do I get Alya back?"

Buzz arched an eyebrow and for a horrifying second, Elle thought she was going to say there was no fixing this, there was no chance. But Buzz's smile spread.

"I think you know that," she said quietly. "I think you already know, Elle."

Chapter Thirty Two

It occurred to her, as she slowly slid the key into the lock, that sneaking into her own apartment was ridiculous. Not only that, but it was well after ten. Shoshannah would be safely tucked up in bed with a satisfyingly gory read. So she really didn't have to worry about sneaking around at all.

Perhaps it was just becoming a habit. The late nights in the office, the early mornings, the tip-toeing around. And she felt guilty for it, she truly did. On the other hand, she really didn't know if she could face a conversation with her grandmother about her private life.

Not this time.

She was doing all she could to bury her feelings, to squash them away in the back of her brain where they might hurt less. And talking with Shoshannah would simply dig them all up again. And what was the point of that?

She'd learned her lessons, she'd made her mistakes, and she wouldn't repeat the situation. She would trust her gut and no one else.

Maybe she'd just needed a reminder of that. Perhaps this was all some big life lesson.

She closed the front door behind her silently, slipping off her shoes and creeping through the entrance hall.

"Alya."

It wasn't a question. Her grandmother wasn't worried that someone else was in the apartment. It was a recognition, an order almost. Alya's heart sank and her pulse quickened. Shit.

She forced herself to smile and casually stroll into the kitchen.

"Can't sleep, Bubbe?" she asked kindly.

But her grandmother was still fully dressed and standing by the stove.

"Sit down," Shoshannah said in a voice that brooked no argument.

Alya wasn't a child, but she was far too sensible to disobey her grandmother when she spoke like that. She sat, and Shoshannah placed a steaming bowl of soup in front of her, dumplings bobbing on the top.

"Bubbe, you should be in bed," she started.

Shoshannah pulled out a chair. "I should," she agreed. "But since you're avoiding me during normal working hours, I supposed that the only way to talk to you was to keep your hours instead."

"I'm not avoiding you!"

"And now you're compounding the problem by lying about it."

Just for a moment, Alya had a glimpse of the younger woman her grandmother used to be, the woman who had braided her hair and grounded her and hugged her when she'd had a bad day. She picked up her spoon.

"I'm sorry," she muttered.

"Eat. Go ahead. You need to eat." Shoshannah watched as Alya took a mouthful. "I understand, Bubbale. I do," she said when Alya had swallowed. "But you can't put off talking about all this forever. It will eat you up inside. Honestly, it will."

"I just—" Alya shook her head. "I just keep hoping it'll all go away if I don't talk about it. If I don't let myself feel it then I won't have to feel it."

"Something is bothering me. I've given you two weeks, longer even, I know you needed some time to yourself. But I can't not ask anymore, Bubbale. I need to know. Who taught you that there are no happy endings? Whoever told you that?"

Alya laughed bitterly. "No one had to tell me. I saw it all the time. My mother was the perfect example."

Shoshannah sighed. "Your mother never sticks around long enough for there to be a happy ending. If she did, maybe she'd finally get one. But it breaks my heart that you would believe that, that you'd think that there was no... no beauty in this world, no true love, no happiness."

Alya took another mouthful of the soup, warm and filling and comforting. "How can you say that?" she said after swallowing. "You sit here, grandfather gone for, what, thirty years now? And you're going to tell me that love stories have happy endings?"

The sound made Alya jump so hard that soup spilled from her bowl. Her grandmother's hand quivered on the table-top where it had smacked down so hard that the room echoed with the sound of it.

"How dare you?"

Alya swallowed, leaning back, afraid almost of the anger in her grandmother's face.

"How dare you say that to me?" Shoshannah said again.

"I—I didn't mean..." But Alya didn't know what she had meant.

Shoshannah put her other hand on the table. She looked older now, tired. "You don't know everything, Alya. You're a clever girl, always have been. Except when it came to yourself. Except when it came to matters of the heart. I had my happy ending, Alya. And I treasure it close to my heart every single day."

"Grandmother..." She put one of her hands on top of one of Shoshannah's.

"I loved my Saul with all my heart. And yes, he's gone, and yes for a long time there I didn't want to go on without him. It was like having my heart ripped out of my body. But what was the alternative? Never loving him at all? Never marrying him at all? We had twenty one years together. Twenty one years filled with love and happiness and a perfection so great it fills my heart to remember it."

Alya could barely remember her grandfather. She had a faint memory of the smell of pipe smoke, of a rough beard. But that was all.

"My happy ending is those memories, Alya. My happy ending is knowing that I had love, that I had pure happiness, and that every time

I close my eyes I can feel it again." She picked up her other hand, patted Alya's. "Just because an ending isn't perfect doesn't mean that it's not happy. Perhaps that's your mother's problem. She's always searching for perfection that doesn't exist."

Alya ate some more soup.

"You've been hurt," Shoshannah said. "But that doesn't mean that you'll get hurt the next time. You have to risk and risk and risk again, or you achieve nothing. You can't stop looking for your happy ending, because if you do then you'll never find it."

"Hurt?" Alya said, putting her spoon down finally. "Elle lied to me. She pretended to be someone she wasn't. She wrote an entire magazine article about me. She snuck into my life and took what she needed to build what she wanted."

"And you fell in love with her."

The words were bold and loud and terrifying. Alya could only stare at her grandmother.

"Bubbale, you can't hide things from me. It was early days, certainly, but I could tell. There was a connection there. There still is, perhaps. If there weren't, then all of this wouldn't hurt so much now, would it?"

And then the tears came. The truth of it, the importance of it, washed over her and for the first time, Alya let her emotions go. It hurt so badly that she wanted to scream with the pain. And her grandmother held her, cradling her head as she sobbed.

It seemed like a long time until she could breathe again, until she was hiccuping quietly, but the tears had stopped flowing.

"So," Shoshannah said. "What now?"

Alya shook her head. "Now nothing. Now, I learn from my mistakes."

Shoshannah looked at her. "We all make mistakes, don't we?"

"Of course."

"There's no perfection, certainly. And we all make mistakes. We all judge things wrongly or think that we want something that we don't.

Or perhaps we prioritize our jobs over our personal lives. Or maybe we lie and then get pulled into a spiral of events we can't control."

Alya straightened up. "I get it, I get what you're trying to say, Bubbe, but—"

"But what? This Elle, she can't make mistakes? She's the only one that is expected to be perfect?"

"Bubbe, she lied to me. She took my privacy from me. She wasn't ever the person I thought she was. Even her name was fake."

"But what if she was the person you thought she was?" pushed Shoshannah. "What if, okay, she made mistakes, she started out trying to get her story, but then, when she met you, she really did start having feelings for you? What then?"

Alya took a deep breath. What then? Then nothing. She couldn't see past what Elle had done. How could she?

Shoshannah patted her hand again. "Think on it, little one. Think about what is more important."

"Some things are unforgivable."

"Forgiveness is a choice," said Shoshannah. "You choose it or you choose to withhold it."

Alya said nothing to this.

"Will you promise me one thing?" her grandmother asked.

"What?"

"Just promise me that you won't give up. There's a happy ending for you, Alya. And I want you to have it. Maybe it's with Elle, maybe it's not. But please, don't stop looking."

But Alya couldn't answer. She bit her lip as her grandmother dropped a kiss on her forehead, and then took herself off to bed.

Chapter Thirty Three

She'd miss the view from Kim's office window, she thought idly. It was familiar to her now. The first time she'd seen that view her heart had beat hard and she'd thought that she'd finally found her place in the world.

Now, of course, she knew that she'd been wrong. The only problem was persuading Kim of that.

"If it's a pay rise you're looking for, that can be negotiated," Kim was saying.

"No, that's not it," said Elle, as patiently as she could. "I don't need more money. I don't need more vacation time. I don't need more independence or more stories or more anything else. What I need is for you to let me quit. Please."

Was she literally begging to be allowed to not work? She rather thought that she was. Kim was still shaking her head though.

"Why now?" Kim asked. "Why now when you've finally gotten somewhere. I told you when you came back to work that you'd found your stride, that you'd finally made it, finally developed into the kind of journalist I've been looking for. And now you want to quit? Why, Elle?"

Kim didn't often use her first name. In fact, Elle couldn't remember Kim having used it before. A sign of her frustration perhaps. She took a deep breath.

"Because I don't want to be the kind of journalist that you're looking for," she said simply.

Kim scowled. "Is that an insult? Because it certainly sounds like one."

"I lied," Elle said. "I lied about everything."

The scowl deepened. "You're not a journalist?"

"No, I am. I just..." She'd planned on telling the whole truth. But she'd been derailed by the fact that Kim seemed unlikely to let her quit at all.

"You just what?"

"The story. Goldstein. It wasn't arranged. When I pitched it to you it was a last ditch effort to keep my job, it was a shot in the dark. I'd talked to no one, arranged nothing, there was no story when I first told you about it."

Kim laughed, then shrugged. "So you lied, so what? Who cares?"

"I do," Elle said. "I care. I care because I lied about it, then I lied to Alya Goldstein, and then I published a story about her that upset her. I care because... Because I'm not a real journalist, Kim. This isn't the life that I want. I can't go around lying and upsetting people."

"Elle—"

"I have to thank you for giving me a chance. For giving me more than one chance. But I also have to be honest. With you, with myself, with everyone. This isn't the job for me. I thought it was, for a long time, but it's just not. It's not who I am. And you were right, I don't have a nose for a good story. I never did. This one was just a pure fluke."

Kim sat back in her chair. "You've got balls, kid."

"Kim, I quit."

Slowly, reluctantly, Kim nodded.

THE BAR WAS LIT WITH the flickering light of candles and Elle could see Buzz as soon as she walked in. There were already two glasses in front of her.

"I didn't know if we were celebrating or commiserating, but I thought I'd better get the drinks in anyway," Buzz said, as soon as Elle was close enough to hear.

"We're... celebrating, I guess," said Elle, slipping off her coat and hanging it on a hook under the bar. "Although, celebrating me quitting my job seems odd."

"How did Kim-possible take it?"

"As well as can be expected." She picked up her glass, clinked it against Buzz's, and then took a drink.

"I hate to put a damper on the party atmosphere," Buzz said, after drinking from her own glass. "But have you given any thought to what's next here? I mean, I'm the first to support your new honest life, the one where you admit all your mistakes and all that, but there is still the small question of rent to pay."

Elle sighed. "I don't know. I really don't." She looked over at her friend. "I do know that I need to thank you though."

"For what?"

"For telling me the truth, for forcing me to take a good long look at myself. I, uh," she blinked away some surprise tears. "I don't know what I'd do without you, Buzz."

"You'd probably just drive down the wrong road until you drove straight into the ocean," Buzz said.

Elle laughed and shot her tears away. "You may well be right. And you're definitely right about finding a new career, a new meaning. I just, well, I don't really know where to start. I chose journalism because it was the furthest thing that I could think of from medicine."

Buzz took her hand and squeezed it. "I know," she said. "And I know why as well. I know how much it hurt you when your parents turned their backs on you. When they told you it was all just a phase, when, finally, you figured out that they wouldn't love you as you are. It's easy to forget nowadays that not every coming out story has a happy ending."

Elle took a drink.

"But I'm here for you, Elle. Always. Always and forever and I'll support you in whatever it is you decide to do next. Just promise me that this time you're going to choose something you want to do, not just something to spite someone else."

"There's no one left to spite," she said, trying to lighten things. She knew that Buzz was there for her. And she knew that she'd never find the words to tell her how much it meant to her.

"Probably for the best."

"Well, I've got some money in the bank, so I've got a little wiggle room to figure things out, I guess. In the meantime, I've volunteered at that new LGBTQ+ center downtown. It'll keep me busy while I plan my next steps."

"Sounds like a plan," Buzz said, looking impressed. "You're really getting back on your feet, aren't you?"

"Almost," Elle said.

It was true, she felt better. Better maybe because she'd decided. Better because she was facing her own flaws and slowly, slowly coming to terms with them.

"There is something else that I need to do. Something I can't put off for much longer."

"Ah," said Buzz, putting down her glass. "Goldstein?"

Elle nodded.

"Maybe that's not such a great idea," Buzz said. "Opening old wounds and all that. Perhaps you need to move on from this one, chalk it up to experience."

"No," Elle said. "I need to do this."

Buzz sighed. "Elle, you're not thinking that she's going to take you back, are you? Because you can't go around chasing old dreams."

"No, no." She looked down at the counter top. "No," she said again, more quietly. "I just... I need to apologize. Properly. Face to face. No excuses. What I did was wrong and she deserves to know that I know that."

"Think you're ready to handle that?"

What a question. She saw Alya's face every time she closed her eyes. She could imagine her touch, could smell her scent. She was, she knew, as smitten with her as she'd always been. As she'd been from the first second she'd seen her, striding across the foyer at MedSend.

"Maybe not," she admitted. "But it's something that I need to do. For her and for me too."

Buzz nodded. "Alright. Here's a question for you though: How the hell are you going to talk your way into seeing Alya Goldstein, the notoriously private and guarded businesswoman, now that she knows exactly who you are? And, not incidentally, now that you've broken her heart and she hates your guts?"

"Not one to sugar coat things, are you?"

Buzz laughed. "Would you like me to?"

"God no, I need someone to slap me around once in a while and make me look at myself in the mirror."

"So," said Buzz. "My question stands. How the hell do you plan on getting Alya Goldstein to not just agree to see you, but to actually listen to you?"

Elle drained her glass. It was an excellent question. And one that she didn't have an answer to.

"You know, the problem with up-ending your life and deciding you're going to become a better you is the distinct lack of a manual to advise you on how to going about doing that," she said.

"Just think of me as your walking manual," said Buzz, with a grin.

"You think you can come up with a way to get Alya to listen to me?"

"Well, I'm the reason you're wanting to apologize to her in the first place, so it only seems fair that I should help you come up with a plan."

Elle nodded. "Okay then, what are you thinking?"

"Well, first of all, where does she like to go, other than home and work?"

Elle closed her eyes in thought. Alya's face filled her mind and her heart sped up at just the memory of her. It took a second before she could concentrate, before she could really think. Where did Alya go? Nowhere, not really. She was obsessed with work. She went from her apartment to the office and back again.

Except...

Except for one night a week.

Elle's eyes flashed open again. "I know where to find her."

Chapter Thirty Four

It felt odd leaving the office before it was fully dark. But Alya had made a vow to herself that she was going to try harder, that she was going to reclaim her life back. Just because one thing had gone wrong, didn't mean she had to destroy everything. Besides, her grandmother's words kept spinning around in her head.

She was about to go when there was a knock at the door. She pulled it open and found Brian Delane.

"You're leaving," he said, seeing her coat and bag.

"You caught me," she smiled.

"I just wanted to let you know that I've signed off on the beta version of the new site design. It looks pretty good to me, though I'm sure there are going to be hiccups along the way."

"Perfect, great. More importantly, how's Sarah?"

She saw a shadow fleet across his face and almost wished she hadn't asked.

"About as well as can be expected," he said.

"Take all the time you need."

He nodded, tried to smile and thanked her before heading back to the stairwell. She watched him go.

Where was his happy ending? Perhaps his wife would recover, perhaps not. It was in the hands of the doctors now. But would he consider this a happy ending? Would he sacrifice the happiness he'd had with Sarah to be able to skip this part entirely?

She sighed and closed her office door.

Like most kids, she'd grown up on fairytales before graduating to movies and television. She'd grown up with the grand gestures, the surprise singing of a love song in the cafeteria maybe, or printing a billboard to say 'I love you.' The kind of grand gesture that was movie-speak for 'and they'll live happily ever after.'

And she knew, as an adult, that those things rarely, if ever happened. And even when they did happen, they were far from any guarantee that there was going to be a happy ending.

She also knew that her grandmother was worried about her, that she was trying to make her feel better. She could only believe half of what Shoshannah had told her. Except... Except if she had to honestly say that she'd skip the good parts to skip the pain...

She closed her eyes for a second, reliving for a brief moment that night spent in Elle's arms. Would she give up that memory if it meant that she'd never met Elle in the first place? If it meant that she didn't hurt now?

No, she decided.

No, she wouldn't.

Elle had never promised her a happy ending. She'd promised a happy middle, and that's exactly what they'd had, short though it was. Setting aside the journalist side of things, Elle had, in fact, generally proved herself to be a moral person. She hadn't spied for Berger. She had sent the books she promised Shoshannah. It was only the big things that she lied about.

We all make mistakes, Shoshannah had said.

Alya tapped her fingers on the empty assistant desk. We all make mistakes. But some hurt more than others. And some just can't be forgiven. Or could they?

She sighed again and looked down at the empty desk. She really needed to get to work on hiring a new assistant, she really needed the help.

She left the office, went down the elevator, strode through the foyer, and went out into the dimness of the early evening. She turned right and began to walk.

Two steps. Three.

She had to get her life back on track. She had to stop waiting around for a happy ending that she wasn't even convinced existed. She needed to reclaim herself.

Four steps. Five.

She stopped.

Right. She was doing this. She turned on her heel and began walking briskly in the other direction. If she hurried, she'd just about make it before warm-ups started.

"I THOUGHT YOU THREW those stupid things away," hissed Buzz.

"Just as well I didn't really, isn't it?" Elle said, clinging on to the heavy bag with one hand.

"Are you sure that she's going to be here?"

"I think so. I mean, it's the only other place I can think of. Besides, she won't let me into her office or home, and at least here she'll be in one place. She can't exactly run away."

"She can roll away," pointed out Buzz. "And you'll have to chase her, which seems like it could end badly."

Elle laughed through the squirmings of nerves in her stomach. "I'll be fine. I didn't die the last time I was here."

"Beginner's luck," grunted Buzz. She sighed. "You're sure this is the right thing to do."

"Definite," Elle said, and she was. "I'm going to apologize at the very least. And I'm going to be honest."

"Honest?"

"I'm going to ask her to take me back," Elle said. The idea had been growing in her mind. Not the expectation. She knew that Alya almost certainly wouldn't take her back, or have anything to do with her at all. But she had to ask, had to be honest and truthful and real.

"Elle…"

"It's fine. I'm expecting nothing. But I have to do this."

Buzz looked up at the building. "Want me to come inside?"

Elle almost said yes. Having Buzz there cheering her on might make all of this a little better. But she'd made this mess herself, she had to clear it up herself. "No. Thank you, but no."

"Suit yourself," Buzz said. "Call me if you need me?"

"I swear."

Buzz grabbed her, kissed her soundly on both cheeks. "Go on then. I'm proud of you, Elle. Proud of you for admitting your wrongs, and proud of you for wanting to change. You go do your thing. And I'll be there for you whenever you're done."

Elle bit her lip, felt a tear threatening to escape. "I, um, I don't know what I'd do without you."

Buzz grinned. "What's family for?" she said. "Go on then, off you go."

Elle took a deep breath and then walked into the roller rink.

Practice had already started. The sound of wheels on polished wood, the muffled thumps of bodies hitting the ground, the piercing whistle of the coach all echoed through the building. Elle slid into the bleachers, craning her neck, trying desperately to see Alya.

She had to be there.

Just had to.

Her heart was thudding and her mouth was dry and she was almost sure that Alya wasn't there. She was just about to admit defeat, about to back away, when she saw a familiar shape. Her stomach flipped over. Alya was here.

Quickly, with trembling fingers, she untied her shoes, fiddling to get her skates on. She was panicky now, her pulse thudding through her, her legs shaking. It was only now that she realized that she didn't exactly have a plan.

Skates on finally, she looked up. The women were still circling around the rink.

Screw a plan.

She didn't need a plan. All she needed was a captive audience to let her admit her mistakes, to apologize for her wrongs.

All she needed was Alya for thirty seconds.

Slowly, tremulously, she skated her way to the gate of the rink, grasping on to benches when she could, tottering on her wheels when she couldn't.

She saw Alya, calculated the speed that the skaters were flying around the rink. Then, without any further thought, she flung herself out onto the slippery surface.

Either she was lucky or her high school math skills were better than she'd remembered, because she managed to slide directly towards Alya. Alya who hadn't noticed her. Alya who was moving awfully fast. Alya who was only now turning in her direction.

Everything slowed down to a crawl.

She had time to see Alya's beautiful face, time to wonder how she'd survived without seeing her every day, time to realize just how deeply she'd fallen for this woman, time to know suddenly that she would never be complete without her, that she didn't want to be without her.

She had time to see finally that this was what life was supposed to be like. Time to understand finally all those love songs and romantic movies, all those cheesy proposals and weeping widows. Time to know with absolute certainty that she'd found something that she would never forget and couldn't let go of.

She had time to realize that Alya was coming closer and closer. Time to realize that Alya was too close. Time to realize that actually, Alya wasn't slowing down. Alya wasn't stopping at all. Alya was close enough to touch. She had time to open her mouth and scream something.

There was a crash. She knew that much. Sensed the noise before it happened, sensed the contact before it hurt.

And then everything went black.

Chapter Thirty Five

Jesus Christ. This wasn't supposed to happen. Alya's fingers twisted together then untwisted and she shuffled on the uncomfortable plastic chair. Just how had this happened?

One minute she'd been in practice, tearing around the rink. The next minute there was someone standing there, someone yelling something, and she hadn't been able to stop. And now... Now here she was, sterile fluorescent lights buzzing and linoleum underfoot and she didn't even know why she was sitting there except she couldn't let Elle do this alone.

"Hey."

The voice from the bed was croaky and weak, but Alya heard it immediately. Elle's blue eyes were open.

"You're in the hospital," Alya said.

"I'd figured that out," said Elle, voice getting stronger now. "Weird bed, weird lights, smell of antiseptic."

"Great," Alya said, teeth on edge. She stood up. "No brain damage then, that's all I needed to hear." She turned to walk out.

Guilt, that was what had brought her here. Guilt plain and simple.

"Wait," Elle shouted.

She turned back. "What?"

"What exactly happened?"

"You don't remember?"

Elle tried to shake her head, winced, and then said: "No."

Alya sighed. She sat down on the side of the bed. "I was at derby. Suddenly, there was someone in front of me, you as it turned out. You yelled something, I didn't have time to stop, and, well..." She looked down at the white starched sheet. "I hit you."

"Huh."

"Huh? That's all you've got?"

"What did I yell?"

"I didn't hear it clearly," Alya said. "It sounded like you were yelling about, well, about assholes."

Elle grinned. "I'm an asshole."

"Yes, something like that."

"No, I'm an asshole," Elle said. "That's what it was. Definitely. That's what I needed to say. To you. I needed to tell you that I'm an asshole and I needed to say that I'm sorry and that I know words will never be enough to apologize for what I did to you. But I needed to say them anyway. I'm sorry, Alya."

She hadn't thought that anything could make a difference. Not really. But hearing Elle say she was sorry felt like a drip of warm water onto her frozen hands. "You're sorry."

Elle blinked and Alya realized that she was close to tears. "I'm not going to make excuses. I'm not going to try and justify anything. What I did was absolutely and completely wrong. I betrayed you, I betrayed your trust, and you have every right to think that I'm an asshole. Because I am. There is one thing that I never, ever lied about. My feelings for you. You have no reason to believe me, I suppose, but I swear I didn't lie about that."

She didn't know what to say, what to feel. She was close to taking Elle's hand even though her brain was screaming at her not to do it, not to fall for it again, not to trust her, not to believe her. But her heart could remember the touch of her, the feel of her, the taste of her.

"Alya, I..." Elle blinked again and looked away. "I'm supposed to make a big gesture. I'm supposed to sing to you or kill a man for you or fill your office with flowers or something, anything. That's how it's supposed to work."

Even right then, Alya couldn't stop herself biting a smile back. "Kill a man? Really?"

Elle choked a laugh. "Maybe we watch different kinds of movies."

"Sounds like it." But maybe they didn't. Maybe Elle was thinking the same as she was, maybe, just maybe there was something there after all.

"I don't have any grand gesture," Elle said, almost whispering. "All I have is me, lying here, right now, and telling you that I don't want to be without you."

Ice was cracking, breaking, chipping away and Alya wanted to kiss her. She wanted this, desperately and viscerally. She wanted to be with Elle. She'd known since that awful second when she'd felt Elle's body crumple beneath her own on the rink. She wasn't here out of guilt, she was here because she didn't want to be anywhere else, she was here because this was where she needed to be.

"Elle, you broke me. You stole my privacy, you—"

"I'm not a journalist anymore. I quit. Believe it or not, that was the first big story I did. And after, well, I found that the person I was forced to be wasn't who I wanted to be. Not at all. I'm not going to work as a journalist again."

Alya felt lighter, physically lighter. "Elle, I don't know."

"Seeing your face every morning was the greatest thing that ever happened to me."

"What?"

"I thought I had everything figured out. I thought I knew what I wanted. And then I saw you. And suddenly I knew I had to be different, I wanted to be different. I went about things so terribly wrong, I know I did. I got twisted up in my own stories and lies and I hurt you so badly. I was trying to free myself, trying to find a way out that would end up with us together, without you getting hurt, without having to tell you that I'd lied to you."

"A happy ending," Alya said. Her fingers touched Elle's.

"Something like that. Even though you don't believe in them."

Her fingers linked in with Elle's and her heart almost stopped. "I'm starting to be persuaded."

"I'm not promising anything," Elle said. "I'm not asking for anything. Not even forgiveness. All I want is to try again."

"I trusted you. I opened up, I let myself feel."

"And I broke that trust."

"You did," Alya said, honestly. "But you also showed me what it was like to have someone. To believe in something. Even for just a short while. And, well, at the end of the day, what else is there? There are no guarantees in life."

"There should be," Elle said, letting her hand clasp Alya's. "I guarantee that all your secrets are safe with me. I won't out you in public or anything, ever. I'll hide away in the shadows if that's what you need."

Now Alya frowned. "What? Why would you hide away?"

"So that people don't see us together, so that you don't get outed. Your secret's safe with me."

"Secret? But I've been out for as long as I can remember. It's no secret."

Elle was struggling to sit up now. Alya moved to stop her, but her eyes looked clear and she wasn't in visible pain.

"That wasn't your secret? That wasn't what you were trying to hide from journalists?"

"No," Alya said. "Not in the slightest."

"Then what is? What's your secret? What are you hiding by being so mysterious and secretive all the time?" Elle snapped her mouth shut and moaned. "I'm doing it again. That's none of my business. I'm sorry, I'm prying."

Alya raised an eyebrow. "Yes, you were prying," she agreed. "On the other hand, I need to learn to be more open. So in the spirit of openness, I'll tell you."

Elle shifted forward a little.

"There's no secret," Alya said.

"But—"

"But nothing," said Alya. "There's no grand secret. I'm not hiding anything. My only secret is that I like my privacy. I don't see why other people should know about my private life. I'm not a movie star or a public figure, I'm a business woman and I'm trying to help people, that's all."

"That's it?" Elle asked, looking confused.

"That's it," said Alya. She cleared her throat. Elle had apologized. She was owed some honesty. "And I should thank you. For the article. I, uh, I got the investment I needed to buy Berger out. But only because the investor read your profile."

Elle's face lit up. "I helped?"

"You helped."

"Alya, I made mistakes. So many. I have no right to expect anything of you. If you choose to get up and walk out right now, I'll understand. I really will."

She should. She should walk away. Not get involved in this mess again. Not hope for a happy ending that might not come. She stood up and she saw Elle's face fall, saw her bite her lip as she tried to keep her sadness inside.

She should walk away.

But she couldn't. Not without seeing how this played out, not without taking a chance, not without seeing if perhaps, maybe, there might be a happy ending here for the taking. Or at least a happy middle.

"No more lies."

"No more lies," Elle said.

Those eyes were so blue that she could sink into them and swim all day. They were full of hope and promise and sadness all mixed together. And Elle had made mistakes, sure, but then, who hadn't? Alya had locked herself away afraid to be hurt, and in the process had almost missed this, had almost never had the feelings that she was having now. And that was the biggest mistake of all.

She bent and softly, gently brushed Elle's lips with her own. A spark of electricity spiked through her. This, how could this ever be wrong? She leaned into the kiss, felt Elle begin to respond.

There was the sound of someone clearing their throat.

Alya jumped back to see a young doctor, hair sticking up, chart in hand.

"Sorry to interrupt," he said, not looking sorry in the least. "Ms. Baker's test results have all come in fine. There's a chance of concussion, but no major damage."

Alya slid a look at Elle, who looked pale but happy.

"We're happy to let you go," the doctor was saying. "As long as you have someone to stay with. You'll need to be under supervision for the next twenty four hours, just in case."

"I'll call my room-mate," Elle said.

But Alya was already reaching out and taking her hand. "No," she said. "No, you'll come with me."

Because in the end, it's not our mistakes that define us. It's the person that we are. And despite the lying and the sneaking, Elle had proven herself over and over to be a decent person. She'd seen the look on her grandmother's face when she'd picked up the books that Elle had sent her. She'd seen the regret on Berger's face when he'd told her that Elle wouldn't work for him. And she'd learned that Elle thought she was hiding her sexuality, a secret that hadn't appeared in the article at all.

And Elle was pulling her down and their lips were meeting again and this time Alya let herself float free as they kissed. The doctor cleared his throat again, twice, three times, before giving up and leaving them in each others' arms.

Epilogue

A month ago it had sounded like a fantastic plan. A month ago, she'd had only butterflies when thinking about it. Now though, she had big fat elephants stomping around in her stomach. She watched people mill around the room, leaning up against the bar and feeling nauseous.

"You look like you're about to barf," Buzz said, sidling up to her.

"Where have you been?"

"I'm fashionably late," Buzz pouted. "And calm the hell down. Want a drink?"

Elle nodded. Calm the hell down? Just how was she supposed to do that?

"Not a bad set up," Buzz said as she waited for their drinks. "I mean, it's not the party of the year or anything, but it's pretty cool. The music's good."

"It's not supposed to be the party of the year," Elle reminded her. "Alya's company is going public, this is just, I don't know, a celebration. She wants to thank the people that worked so hard for her. It's an excuse to have a good time, that's all."

"I'm just making conversation," Buzz said. "And you're seriously on edge."

"I—" She interrupted herself with a sigh. This was Buzz. "What if I'm making a mistake?"

Buzz laughed. "My love, knowing you, if you were making a mistake, you'd go ahead and do it anyway just to prove a point."

"Not kind."

"I'm only teasing you because you're being silly." Buzz collected their drinks and slid one in front of Elle. "Do you think you're making a mistake?"

Elle shook her head and the elephants stomped in her stomach again.

"There you go then," said Buzz. "Yes, you should definitely try not to screw up, but you should trust your gut sometimes too."

Elle sighed again. That was easier said than done.

"BUBBE! CHAMPAGNE? SERIOUSLY?" Alya swooped onto her grandmother, hand already poised to take the glass away, but Shoshannah was already moving it out of reach.

"Rachel said one glass was fine," Shoshannah said.

But Alya's eyes were fixed on her grandmother's hand. A hand she knew better than her own. A hand that was now older and more wrinkled and more loved, and that was definitely missing something.

"Where's your ring?"

Shoshannah glanced at her hand, reddened slightly, and put the glass down, her hand down by her side. "I must have forgotten it."

"It's your wedding ring, you never take it off."

"Maybe I lost it," Shoshannah said. She didn't sound sad. She was taking Alya's arm. "And now is a good opportunity to tell you that I'm very, very proud of you."

"Bubbe..."

"No, you've done well. I'm proud. Of everything you've done. Your company, your hard-work. And Elle too." Shoshannah squeezed her hand.

"Elle?" Alya glanced over to the bar where Elle was deep in discussion with Buzz.

"You opened yourself up to someone, you took a risk, and I'm prouder of you for that than for anything else. The two of you fit together so well."

Alya bit her lip. She wasn't so sure about that. Elle had been distant for weeks now. She'd put it down at first to the fact that she was busy, working all hours trying to get the plans to go public finished. But now she was beginning to wonder. Maybe things were cooling down, maybe Elle's feelings were changing. It had been a long eighteen months, and she knew there were no guarantees for the future. Her throat ached just thinking about it.

"Now I'm going to mingle," Shoshannah said. "I don't get out as much as I used to. It's nice having someone else to talk to for a change."

"Someone other than me and Elle?" Alya asked, smiling at her grandmother.

"You're damn straight."

Alya grinned, then glanced down at her grandmother's hand again. She'd never seen her without the ring before. It made her look almost naked. "I'll help you look for your ring tomorrow."

"Right," Shoshannah said, already edging away.

Alya watched her go. She knew her grandmother wasn't a young woman, and she carefully never thought about what she'd do when... when circumstances changed. But this, the missing ring, the lack of emotion over something that had been so important to her life, this was new. Maybe Shoshannah wasn't quite as sharp as she used to be. Maybe it was time to admit that.

"Ms. Goldstein?"

She turned to see a member of the press coming toward her. They'd had to be here, she'd had to publicize the event. But that didn't mean she had to talk to them. Quickly, she walked in the opposite direction.

ELLE GULPED DOWN THE rest of her drink, seeing Alya walking toward her. Not that she was planning on doing anything now, not in front of all these people. It had taken a while to get used to Alya's privacy obsession, but she got it now, got that Alya liked having her own private life, not having to share with anyone else.

And to be fair, Alya was improving too. Although from the looks of it she was currently fleeing a photographer, so maybe she wasn't quite on form tonight.

"It's wonderful," Buzz said as Alya approached her and kissed her cheek. "The party of the year."

Elle rolled her eyes, and Alya grinned. "It's a business thing," Alya said. "If I ever need a real party you'll be my first call."

"I'm sorry I didn't see you before you left," Elle said. "I was running late."

"School okay?"

Elle nodded. School was fine. Better than fine. School was filling in a missing piece of her life. After six months of working at the LGBTQ+ center she'd been promoted to a paid staff member. And after a year she'd made the decision to go back to school to get a counseling degree that she hoped was going to put her on track to work with youths like herself who'd had tough coming out stories.

"Perfect," Alya said.

She turned to look at the small stage and Elle found herself tongue-tied by her beauty once again. Tongue-tied and nervous and the elephants started stomping in her stomach and she didn't know what to say. She knew that she was acting strangely, she knew that she was drawing away from Alya. But it was nerves. She just couldn't deal with the thought that maybe Alya would say no.

"I need to get up there and make my speech," Alya said, nodding at the stage. "It's about that time of the evening. Everyone should be drunk enough that I won't make a complete fool of myself."

With a shot of pain Elle suddenly remembered why it had been so important that she was on time today. She'd been supposed to proof-read Alya's speech before they left for the party. She saw now why Alya was being short with her.

"Good luck with that," Buzz was saying as Alya started to walk away.

"Shit," said Elle under her breath.

"Problem?" asked Buzz.

"Yes. No. Maybe. I was an asshole again."

Buzz rolled her eyes. "And what have we learned about being an asshole?"

"That I recognize it and deal with the problem immediately," Elle parroted.

She handed her empty glass to Buzz and ran off, chasing Alya as she disappeared through a door to one side of the stage.

By the time she caught up, Alya was already having a microphone fitted to the front of her long, dark blue dress. A dress that had made Elle's legs weak the first time she'd seen it. When he saw Elle coming, the technician, patted the microphone and walked away, giving them some privacy.

"I'm sorry," Elle said. "I'm really sorry. I totally forgot about the speech and I totally forgot about the time."

"It's fine," Alya said, examining the microphone on her chest.

"It's not fine. I'm an asshole."

Alya sighed. "Elle, you can't just say that every time you do something wrong. You're not an asshole. You were busy. I get it. I get busy too."

"I shouldn't have been too busy for this, it was important."

"Well, you were. And I'm busy too."

Above Elle's head a speaker crackled. The backstage area was small and dark and she could see the light of the stage beaming through a curtain.

"I know you're busy, I..." She bit her lip. "I'm really sorry."

"And I get why you wouldn't make me a priority. I mean, I've been working for weeks on this event and getting the company up and running properly. So I see why you'd want to punish me."

The speaker crackled again. Elle's breath left her lungs. "Punish you? I'm not punishing you."

"Then why are you being like this, Elle? Why are you pulling away from me? I feel like we're losing a connection here."

"What are you talking about?" She took a step closer.

"You know what I'm talking about. You're pulling away from me. You're asleep when I come home, or pretending to be, you can't hold a whole conversation with me, you stare at me strangely every time I walk into a room."

Only then did Elle realize just how strangely she'd been behaving. She honestly hadn't meant it. But every time she looked at Alya she was imagining what was going to happen, what she was going to say. And sometimes it all just got too much for her, she couldn't handle it and didn't know what to say, or had to walk away.

"I'm not pulling away," she said. The speaker crackled more loudly this time.

"You are. And I get it. If you want to leave, if this is a conversation we need to have, then we should have it. Just not now."

"No, I'm not pulling away. I'm just nervous."

"Nervous?" Alya's eyebrows shot up. She laughed. "Nervous? Seriously? You expect me to believe that? You don't have to lie to me, Elle. You never promised me a happy ending, you promised a happy middle. And maybe you're right, maybe we've already had that. But please, please don't lie."

"I'm not lying," Elle protested.

The technician was walking toward Alya and the speaker crackled again, louder than ever and Elle felt the vibrations in her bones.

"Elle, please." Alya just stared at her for a moment, the disappointment in her eyes clear. And then she turned to walk away.

"I'm just nervous!" Elle called after her.

But Alya was walking away and the speaker was crackling louder and louder and Elle saw her future leaving her and she was damned if she was making a mistake like that again. She ran, flinging herself toward Alya, grabbing hold of her arms, forcing her to turn and face her.

"I'm just nervous Alya because I want to ask you to marry me and I'm terrified that you're going to say no and Alya I love you with all of my heart and please, please don't say no."

Her words had an echoing quality that she heard as soon as they came out of her mouth but she was too caught up in the moment to understand why. And then her mouth clamped shut and there was a resounding cheer from the party behind them, a loud round of applause starting and whistles and Elle's eyes dropped and she saw the microphone pinned to Alya's dress and...

She ran.

WHAT HAD SHE DONE? Her perfect proposal, all planned out, and she'd just let it slip like that. And it had been heard by hundreds of people. Her proposal to the most private person in the world. Alya was never going to forgive her.

She was sobbing now and knew that make-up had to be running down her face and she didn't know where to go, what to do. She just knew that she'd screwed everything up. It was supposed to be a private moment, a personal moment, and she'd invited everyone at the event into it. Alya must be fuming.

She found the ladies room, slammed open the door and went in, clutching at the edge of the cool sink, taking deep breaths and trying to control herself. In the mirror she could see mascara stains on her cheeks and that provoked even more tears. Great, not only had she just practically guaranteed that there was no way Alya was going to marry her, but she was going to add to the embarrassment by looking like a drunk girl at prom.

She pulled a paper towel out of the dispenser, wet it, and with vicious strokes wiped away the smeared make-up.

She could hear more applause from the hall. Alya must be giving her speech. Shit.

No, she wasn't running away. As much as she wanted to slip out of a back door and into the cold night she was going to stay. She was going to support Alya, come what may.

Her legs were shaking as she walked out of the bathroom and slid into the back of the hall. In the spotlight, Alya stood, dark hair gleaming.

"There are so many thanks to give," she was saying. "And I know that I couldn't have done this without all of you. Taking MedSend public has been one of the proudest days of my career. But there are a couple of people that I do need to personally thank."

Elle blinked away tears again. She'd really screwed things up this time, she realized.

"One of those is my grandmother, who has always believed in me and supported me and who was one of MedSend's very first customers."

There was a polite round of applause and Elle looked around and could see Shoshannah beaming at the front of the crowd. Shoshannah who had been so supportive, who had been in on the plan from the start, who had surrendered her wedding ring to Elle's care saying that she'd just been waiting for someone who cared enough to love her grand-daughter forever.

A ring she'd need to give back now.

"And the second of those people is my fiancée."

There was a rumble of laughter and Elle looked up, sure she'd misheard.

"I'm sure you all overheard what was accidentally broadcast over the speakers," Alya continued. "And whilst I appreciate your congratulations, I have to tell you that you're not all invited to the wedding." More laughter. "But Elle Baker, the love of my life and a woman that ran away before I could even say yes, wherever you are right now, I want to thank you. And to tell you that I'd be honored to be your wife."

Elle had no idea what happened for the next few minutes. Not a single memory. There was a blur of people and words and feelings and her heart pounded a deep rhythm and she knew nothing at all for certain until Alya was taking her hand and leading her away and out into the corridor.

"I—I'm sorry," she managed to stutter.

But Alya was pulling her closer, letting her arms wrap around her waist. "No need to be sorry. You didn't know the microphone had been switched on."

"No, I'm sorry for it not being more perfect, sorry for it not being private, and sorry for acting like an ass over the last couple of weeks. I was just so nervous and—"

"And nothing, Elle. Yes, you've been acting like an ass. But you're my ass, and I love you."

She looked up and got caught in Alya's green eyes. "You do?"

"With all my heart and more besides. And I'm sorry that I haven't been around more. If I had, maybe I'd have noticed that you were feeling stressed, maybe we would have communicated better."

"It wasn't exactly the best proposal in the world."

"It was perfect," Alya said, stroking her hair. "Well, except for the lack of ring, I think that part is kind of traditional, isn't it?"

Elle felt her face flush red. The ring, she'd completely forgotten about it. "Hold on," she stuttered. She opened up her clutch, rooting through it until she found the precious band of gold. "I, um, was planning on giving you this tonight. Up on the roof. After the party when it was just you and I. I had a whole speech prepared and everything." She held up the ring.

"Elle, that... It's... I don't know what to say."

"Shoshannah gave it to me, with her blessing," Elle said, afraid for a second that Alya might get the wrong impression.

"And I thought she was losing her mind, misplacing her wedding ring like that," Alya said quietly.

With trembling hands, Elle slid the ring onto Alya's finger. "You sure you want to say yes to this?"

Alya looked at her and Elle couldn't think of anyone she'd rather be with, anyone she'd rather talk to or sing with or feed or lie next to at night.

"I'm absolutely sure," Alya said.

"But there aren't supposed to be any happy endings," Elle reminded her. "No fairy tale weddings, not grand gestures."

"Who said we're having a fairy tale wedding," said Alya, drawing closer.

"I've already booked the carriage and horses," Elle said.

She didn't tease any longer because Alya was already brushing her lips against her mouth, was already sliding a tongue curiously into her mouth, was already pulling her in so that their bodies molded together and Elle lost all her breath.

SHE'D HOPED TO GET back into the party unnoticed, but there was no way that was happening. She was the one being celebrated tonight, and her engagement to Elle had done nothing more than excite the press photographers.

And she couldn't run away much longer.

As they walked back in, Elle took her hand and Alya decided that she needed to feed the press a bone. She stopped and they both turned toward the flashing camera. Alya smiled, but she couldn't help smiling with Elle's hand in hers. She couldn't believe that she'd actually thought Elle was going to leave her. And now, well, now they'd be together for as long as they had.

"Can we get a comment?" shouted a journalist.

Alya just smiled, putting an arm around Elle's waist. There was no need to go overboard with the publicity.

"Maybe a short interview?" shouted someone else.

Alya swallowed, but kept her smile. It was Elle that pulled away, Elle that steered her out of the range of the photographers and journalists. The pictures would hit the papers in the morning, but that was just fine. She'd learned to compromise a little with publicity, learned that it could be helpful, that she didn't always need to be mysterious.

"I'll get us some champagne," whispered Elle in her ear, her voice full of the promise of what was to come later in the evening.

Alya shivered and nodded.

She took a seat as she waited for Elle to come back and didn't notice her grandmother until Shoshannah was sitting next to her.

"Congratulations, Bubbale."

"You knew all about this," Alya said, accusatory.

"Guilty," said Shoshannah, but she was smiling. "And I'm not one bit sorry for it."

Alya swallowed, seeing Elle's figure over at the bar. "Do you think I'm doing the right thing?" she asked.

"I do."

Alya reached out and took her grandmother's hand. "Are you always right?" she asked.

"Mostly," Shoshannah said. "I've learned a fair few things in my time."

"Like what?"

Shoshannah smiled at her and through the crowd she could see Elle coming back, champagne flutes in her hands.

"Like that every real story has a happy ending," Shoshannah said.

Alya smiled, her heart so full she thought it might burst. "Yes," she said. "I think you might be right about that."

Thanks for Reading!

If you liked this book, why not leave a review? Reviews are so important to independent authors, they help new readers discover us, and give us valuable feedback. Every review is very much appreciated.

And if you want to stay up to date with the latest Sienna Waters news and new releases, then sign up for my newsletter[1], or follow me on Twitter[2] or on Facebook[3]!

1. http://eepurl.com/dOyZBv

2. https://twitter.com/WatersSienna

3. https://www.facebook.com/Sienna-Waters-321525678594826/

Don't miss out!

Visit the website below and you can sign up to receive emails whenever Sienna Waters publishes a new book. There's no charge and no obligation.

https://books2read.com/r/B-A-SVLH-XIJKB

BOOKS 2 READ

Connecting independent readers to independent writers.

Also by Sienna Waters

The Opposite of You
The Real Story
A Big Straight Wedding
Love By Numbers
The Life Coach

Watch for more at https://www.siennawaters.com/.

About the Author

I've always loved romance, any kind of romance. But growing up, I could never find the exact kind of romance I wanted, the kind of romance about people like me. So I decided to write it myself. My books are about two people falling in love, just like all romances are. But in my case, those two people just happen to both be women. And all my stories have a happy ending, because I truly believe that there's a happy ending out there waiting for everyone.

When I'm not writing I'm spending far too much time online shopping, trying to persuade my cats to dress up, and trying to persuade my wife that I'm not as crazy as I sometimes appear (she believes this about half the time, the other half of the time she just puts up with me with endless patience).

If you'd like to know more about me, or you'd like to stay up to date with new releases, then subscribe to my newsletter here: http://eepurl.com/dOyZBv

Thank you for reading!

Read more at https://www.siennawaters.com/.